The rich tones that still had the power to send her heart on a drumroll and little pops of awareness sparking along her every nerve-ending belonged to a man she had truly believed she would never see again.

Iris stopped and stared.

Asad looked back at her, his dark gaze so intense she felt the breath leave her lungs in a gasp.

Despite his European designer suit and their civilized surroundings, he looked like a desert warrior. Capable. Confident. *Dangerous*.

His brown eyes stayed fixed firmly on her. Serious and probing. The humor that had used to lurk there was nowhere in evidence. He'd filled out since university days too—his body more muscled, his presence every bit that of a man of definite power. At six feet three inches he had always been a presence hard to ignore, but now...?

He was a true warrior.

Wish............ ....that she *could*
ig..ine her
h...

Lucy Monroe started reading at the age of four. After she'd gone through the childrens' books at home, her mother caught her reading adult novels pilfered from the higher shelves on the bookcase…alas, it was nine years before she got her hands on a Mills & Boon® romance her older sister had brought home. She loves to create the strong alpha males and independent women who people Mills & Boon books. When she's not immersed in a romance novel (whether reading or writing it), she enjoys travel with her family, having tea with the neighbours, gardening, and visits from her numerous nieces and nephews.

Lucy loves to hear from her readers: e-mail LucyMonroe@LucyMonroe.com, or visit www.LucyMonroe.com

Recent titles by the same author:

FOR DUTY'S SAKE
THE GREEK'S PREGNANT LOVER
THE SHY BRIDE

**Did you know these are also available as eBooks?
Visit www.millsandboon.co.uk**

HEART OF A
DESERT WARRIOR

BY
LUCY MONROE

First published in Great Britain 2011
by Mills & Boon, an imprint of Harlequin (UK) Limited.
Harlequin (UK) Limited, Eton House, 18-24 Paradise Road,
Richmond, Surrey TW9 1SR

© Lucy Monroe 2012

ISBN: 978 0 263 89088 4

Harlequin (UK) policy is to use papers that are natural, renewable and recyclable products and made from wood grown in sustainable forests. The logging and manufacturing process conform to the legal environmental regulations of the country of origin.

Printed and bound in Spain
by Blackprint CPI, Barcelona

HEART OF A
DESERT WARRIOR

For Helen Bianchin…
it is said that good writing inspires good writers.

Your writing has inspired me
both in my life and in writing for years.

I thank you from the bottom of my heart
for the many hours of pleasurable reading,
the wonderful bits of advice and kind words
when I was the new kid on the block.

Your stories continue to inspire,
your books are my dear friends and
your characters beloved to my heart. Thank you.

CHAPTER ONE

"YOU LOOK like you're ready to face a firing squad."

Her field assistant's words stopped Iris at the top of the grand palace staircase.

Suppressing a grimace at what she could not doubt was his all too accurate assessment, she turned to face the college intern and forced a smile. "*You* look hungry."

"Seriously, this is just dinner right?"

"Of course." Just dinner.

Where they were supposed to meet their liaison while in Kadar; Asad, Sheikh Hakim's second cousin, or something, and sheikh himself to a local Bedouin tribe, the Sha'b Al'najid. Asad was a fairly common Arabic name, meaning lion. An appropriate name for a man destined to be sheikh. Right? There was no reason to think that the man was *her* Asad.

No reason other than this awful sinking feeling that had not gone away since Sheikh Hakim had mentioned the liaison's name earlier. Ever since agreeing to this Middle Eastern assignment, she'd had a feeling of foreboding that she'd done her best to ignore.

But it was getting harder with every passing moment.

"I'm not feeling reassured here," Russell said as

he stepped onto the stairs, his tone only half joking. "Dinner isn't a euphemism for *kidnap and sell to white slavers,* is it?"

The ridiculous assertion shocked a laugh out of Iris. "You're an idiot."

Still, her legs refused to move.

"But a charming one. You've got to admit it. And who wouldn't want to kidnap this?" he asked with a wink, having stopped to wait for her.

With his shaggy mop of red hair and pale skin, he could have been her baby brother. If only. Her childhood would have been a lot less lonely with a sibling. Her parents hadn't been cruel, only supremely uninterested. Their lives were complete with each other. They worked together, they played together, they traveled together and none of it included her.

She'd never understood why they'd had a child at all and had long since decided her advent into the world had been one of those "accidents" of faulty birth control. Though nothing had ever been said.

She couldn't imagine what they would have done with a child like Russell; he didn't fade into the background with grace.

No, no matter how many surface resemblances they shared, he would have been an even bigger cuckoo in their family nest than she'd been.

Nevertheless, Iris and Russell really did look like they could have come from the same gene pool. Oh, he had freckles and she didn't, and his eyes were green rather than her blue. However, they both had curly red hair—like her mother—slightly squared chins—like her father—and skin as pale as the white sands of New Mexico. At five foot ten, Russell was average height for a man, just like she was for a woman at five-five.

They both tended to dress like the science geeks they were, though tonight she'd donned a vibrant blue sheath dress and a black pashmina. Instead of her usual ponytail, she'd pulled her hair back in a loose knot and even gone so far as to put on mascara and lipstick, though she almost never wore makeup. She was dining with a sheikh and his family after all.

Two sheikhs, her worried brain reminded her.

Russell was in his own version of dress formal, khaki slacks and a button-down oxford instead of his usual T-shirt and cargo pants.

Still, neither of them were all-that-and-a-bag-of-chips.

She groaned at his humorous conceit. "Anyone with half a brain would know better than to go through the trouble of kidnapping you."

He laughed, not taking offense and not entirely masking a concerned expression she didn't want to see.

No matter what, she would be fine. She *would.* She was no longer a naive university sophomore, but a professional geologist with an eminent private survey firm.

"So, why the long face?" Russell asked, taking another step down as if coaxing her to do the same. "I know you tried to get out of doing this assignment."

She had, but then she'd realized how foolish she was being. She couldn't go through her career refusing lucrative assignments in the Middle East just because she'd once loved a man who came from this part of the world. Besides, her boss had made it clear that this time, she didn't have a choice.

"I'm fine. Just a little jet-lagged." Forcing her feet to move, she started down the stairs.

Russell fell into step beside her when she reached him. He put his arm out for her and she took it.

She wasn't dwelling on the possibility that Sheikh Asad was *her* Asad. Not at all.

After all, what were the chances it was the same man who had done such a good job decimating her heart six years ago that she hadn't gone on another date until after she graduated? That it was the one man that she had hoped to live the whole rest of her life without ever seeing again?

Small. Almost nonexistent.

Right? *Right.*

So, her Asad had been part of a Bedouin tribe and, as she'd found out at the end, slated to be sheikh one day.

It didn't have to be the same man. *She was praying it wasn't the same man.*

If it was *her* Asad—or rather *the* Asad: he'd never really been hers and she had to stop thinking of him that way—she didn't know what she would do. Working toward the coveted position of senior geologist with Coal, Carrington & Boughton Surveyors, Inc., she couldn't refuse this assignment based on personal reasons. Not when she had been back in the office and definitely not now that she was already in the country.

She wasn't about to commit career suicide. Asad had taken enough from her. Her faith in love. Her belief in the rosy, bright future she'd ached for and dreamed of. He didn't get her career, too.

"What did the diamond say to the copper vein?" Russell's youthful voice pulled her out of her less than happy thoughts as they made their slow way down the stairs.

She rolled her eyes. "That joke is as old as the bedrock in Hudson Bay. The answer is—nothing, minerals don't *talc*."

It was a hoary old joke, but when he laughed, she found herself joining him.

"I'm glad to see you still have a sense of humor." The deep voice coming from the hall below didn't sound happy at all.

In fact, it sounded almost annoyed. But Iris didn't have the wherewithal to worry about that little inconsistency. Not when the rich tones that still had the power to send her heart on a drumroll and to spark little pops of awareness along her every nerve ending belonged to a man she had truly believed she would never see again.

She stopped her descent and stared. Asad looked back at her, his dark chocolate gaze so intense, she felt the breath leave her lungs in a gasp.

He'd changed. Oh, he was still gorgeous. His hair still a dark brown, almost black and with no hint of gray, but instead of cropped close to his head like it had been back in school he wore it shoulder length. The different style should have made him seem more casual, more approachable. It didn't.

Despite his European designer suit and their civilized surroundings, he looked like a desert warrior. Capable. Confident. *Dangerous*.

His brown eyes stayed fixed firmly on her. Serious and probing. The humor that used to lurk there nowhere in evidence.

He had close-cropped facial hair that only added to his appeal, as if he needed any help in that department. He'd filled out since university days, too, his body more muscled, his presence every bit that of a man of definite power. At six feet three inches, he had always been a presence hard to ignore, but now? He was a true Middle Eastern sheikh.

Wishing, not for the first time, that she *could* ignore

this man, she forced herself to incline her head in greeting. "Sheikh Asad."

"This is our liaison?" Russell croaked, reminding her that he was still there.

It didn't help. The young intern was no competition for her attention to Asad and the feelings roiling up from the depths where she'd buried them when he left her.

Putting his arm out to Iris, Asad showed no sign of noticing Russell at all. "I will escort you to the others."

Her frozen limbs unstuck and Iris managed to descend the remaining stairs. Giving in to her urge to ignore at least his suggestion, she stepped around his extended arm and headed to where she'd met earlier with Sheikh Hakim, his wife and their adorable children. If she was lucky, the dining room would be in the same part of the palace.

"Do you know where you are going?" Russell asked from behind her, sounding confused.

Asad made a sound that almost sounded like amusement. "I do not believe Iris has ever let a lack of certainty stop her from going forward."

She spun around and faced him, long-banked fury unexpectedly spiking and with it not a little pain. "Even the best scientist can misinterpret the evidence." Taking a deep breath, she regained the slip in her composure and asked with frigid politeness, "Perhaps you would like to the lead the way?"

Once again, he offered his arm. Again she pushed the bounds of polite behavior and ignored it, simply waiting in silence for him to get on with showing them where they were going.

"Just as stubborn as you ever were."

And she wanted to smack him, which shocked her

to her core. She was not a violent person. Ever. Even in the past, when he'd hurt her almost beyond bearing, she'd never had a violent thought toward him. Just pain.

"That's our Iris, as immovable as a monolith."

Asad didn't ignore Russell this time. He gave the younger man a look meant to quell.

Seemingly oblivious, the college intern grinned and put his hand out to shake. "Russell Green, intrepid geological assistant, one day to be a full-fledged senior geologist with my own lab."

Asad shook the younger man's hand and inclined his head slightly. "Sheikh Asad bin Hanif Al'najid. I will be your team's guide and protector while you are in Kadar."

"Personally?" Iris asked, unable to keep her disquiet out of her voice. "Surely not. You are a sheikh."

"It is a favor to my cousin. I would not consider relegating the duty to someone else."

"But that's unnecessary." She wasn't going to survive the next few weeks if she had to spend them in his company.

It had been six years since the last time she'd seen this man, but the pain and sense of betrayal he'd caused felt as fresh as if it had happened only the day before. Time was supposed to heal all wounds, but hers were still bleeding hurt into her heart.

She still dreamed about him, though she called the images she woke to in the dark nightmares rather than dreams.

She'd loved and trusted him with everything inside her, believing she finally had a shot at a family and a break from the loneliness of her upbringing. He'd betrayed both her emotions and her hopes completely and irrevocably.

"It is not up for discussion."

Iris shook her head. "I…no…"

"Iris, are you okay?" Russell asked.

But she had to be okay. This was her job. Her career, the only thing she had left in her life that mattered, or that she could trust.

The only thing Asad's betrayal had left her with. "I'm fine. We need to join Sheikh Hakim."

Something glimmered in Asad's dark chocolate gaze, something that looked like concern. She wasn't buying it, not even if someone else gave her the money to do it.

He hadn't been concerned about her six years ago when they had been lovers; it was too far a stretch to think he was worried about her now, when they were little more than strangers with a briefly shared past.

Asad did not offer his arm again, but turned and began walking in the direction she'd been going to begin with.

So she had guessed right in this instance.

Go her. Sometimes her intuitive thoughts were on target, at least when it didn't come to people.

"So Asad tells us you went to the same university." Catherine smiled without malice, genuine interest shining in her gentian-blue eyes.

Nevertheless, the memories her words evoked were not happy ones for Iris. Iris forced something that resembled a smile and a nod. "Yes."

"It's funny you should have met."

At the time Iris had believed it destiny. She'd been studying Arabic as her second language, a common practice for those in her field, but it had felt like more. Studying the language of his birth had felt like a common bond between them, as if they were meant to be together.

She had believed him to be an incredible blessing after nineteen years of feeling like she never really belonged to, or with, anyone. She'd thought she'd belonged to Asad; she'd been convinced he belonged to her.

She'd been spectacularly wrong. He didn't want her, not for a lifetime, or even beyond their few months together. And he was not hers, not in any sense.

"It was one of those things...." Asad had come on to her in the Student Union. He'd flirted, charmed and when he asked her out, she hadn't even considered saying no.

"The Student Union building knew no class distinctions," Asad added when it was clear Iris wasn't going to say anything else.

"Not in age or social standing," Russell agreed. "I met a billionaire's daughter in the Student Union at my university."

And Iris had met a sheikh. Not that she'd known it. Back then, he'd just been plain Asad Hanif to her. Another foreign student availing himself of an American university education.

"She was sweet," Russell continued, "but she doesn't know the difference between sedimentary and igneous rock."

"So, not a friendship destined to prosper," Sheikh Hakim observed, his tone tinged with undeniable humor.

"*Our* friendship prospered." Asad gave her a look as if expecting Iris to agree, even after the way their *friendship* had ended. "Though I knew little of geology and Iris had no more interest in business management."

"The friendship didn't last, which would indicate our differences were a lot more important than they seemed at first." She'd managed to say it without a trace of bitterness or accusation.

Iris had never really considered herself much of an actress, but she was channeling Kate Winslet with her performance tonight. She'd managed to get through predinner drinks and the first course of their meal without giving away the turmoil roiling inside her to her hosts, the Sheikh of Kadar and his wife, *just Catherine please*.

Asad laid his fork across his empty salad plate. "Youth often lacks wisdom."

"You were five years older than me." And worlds wiser and more experienced.

He shrugged, that movement of his shoulders she knew so well. It was his response to anything for which there was no good, or easy to articulate, answer.

"Anyway, I hope my words haven't made it seem I'm looking to renew any old friendships." Chills of horror rolled down her spine at the thought. "I'm not. I'm here to work." It was her turn to shrug, though it was more a jerk of one shoulder.

She'd never done casual well when it came to Asad, but it didn't matter. She *was* in Kadar to work and then she would be out of his life once again, just as fully and completely as before. As she was sure he would prefer.

And she was never returning to Kadar. Not ever. No matter how lucrative a promotion depended on it.

"It would be a shame to travel so far from your home and spend no time experiencing the local culture." Asad's gaze bored into hers with predatory intent.

She remembered that look and her heart tightened at receiving it here, in this place, after everything that had passed between them and in his life particularly since their breakup.

"I'm sure living amidst your tribe will give both Iris and Russell the perfect opportunity to experience much of our culture," Catherine said with a smile aimed first at Asad and then Iris. "I love staying with the Bedouin. It's such a different way of life. Though why it always seems there's more trouble for our children to get into in the city of tents than at home, I don't know."

She winked at her husband and Sheikh Hakim gave her such a look of love and adoration, it was both wonderful and painful to see. Here was a couple who loved each other every bit as much as Iris's parents, but who adored their offspring with equal, if different, intensity.

Then the full import of Catherine's words hit Iris. "We're staying with Sheikh Asad's tribe?" she asked in shock. "But I thought *this* would be our home base."

The beautiful Middle Eastern palace that still managed to feel like a home for all its glamour and size.

"Our current encampment is far closer to the mountainous region you will be surveying," Asad said, an inexplicable tone of satisfaction lacing his words.

CHAPTER TWO

"STAYING WITH the Sha'b Al'najid will save you a lot of time in travel," Sheikh Hakim added.

"But…"

"You'll love it, trust me," Catherine said. "While Asad has taken the tribe in a different direction than Hakim's grandfather did, their way of life has much in common with that found millennia ago. It will be an amazing experience, believe me."

Iris would be in purgatory, but at least the encampment would only be their home base, she tried to tell herself. "I'm sure I will enjoy it very much," she lied through her teeth. "What time we spend there, at any rate."

Catherine looked inquiringly. "I'm not sure I understand."

"When we're in the field doing the type of survey Kadar has requested of CC&B, a team spends most of its time in a portable camp," Iris explained. "It really wouldn't make much of a difference if we maintained a home base here, or in the Bedouin encampment."

"You are not staying alone in a camp with nothing but this pup for company." Asad's voice, laced with possessive bossiness, brooked no argument.

And shocked Iris to the core. She didn't understand

why it mattered to him. And that possessiveness was completely at odds with a man already taken himself. She must have imagined it.

The first to admit that reading people was not her strong suit, she nevertheless felt a shiver of apprehension skate along her spine.

"It's not as if we share a cot, just a tent," Russell said, no doubt trying to assuage any conservative sensibilities.

And doing a really bad job of it, Iris thought.

Asad's features set in a mask she was sure had more in common with his warrior ancestors than modern man. He gave Russell a look that made her self-defined intrepid field assistant shrink into his chair.

"Not acceptable." Just two words, but spoken with absolute authority in a tone she'd heard only once from Asad.

When he was telling her they had no future in words that could not be denied.

Russell squeaked. Catherine's look tinged with concern. Iris's heart ached with memory while she fought to maintain a facade of indifference.

Sheikh Hakim frowned. "My cousin is correct. It would be neither safe, nor appropriate for you to camp in such a manner."

Iris could see her escape route disappearing in front of her eyes while the chilly sense of dread inside her grew. She couldn't give up without a fight, though. "I assure you, I've been on several field assignments, in the States and abroad, and never had a problem with it."

Just not in the Middle East.

"Nevertheless, I am responsible for the safety of those within my borders," Sheikh Hakim said with a shake of his head. "Asad is right, a two-person camp in the mountains is an unacceptable option."

Asad simply looked at her with an immovable expression she would never forget. He'd used it also when he said goodbye. "As I told you earlier, I will see to your safety."

"My safety isn't your responsibility."

"On the contrary. I have decreed that it is." Sheikh Hakim's friendly manner dissipated in the face of his arrogant assurance.

Right. And Sheikh Hakim was a very important client. His country was paying CC&B a great deal of money for this survey. She was compelled to accept the way he wanted the field work handled. Either she backed out of the assignment, or accepted the constraints surrounding it, including Asad as her liaison.

She'd accepted that backing out of the assignment wasn't an option before she ever left the States.

"Not having a moving camp could make the initial sample gathering and measurements take significantly longer," she said by way of her final sally.

"Swift is not always better," Sheikh Hakim said implacably. "Your safety must come first."

"Would you be more comfortable with a male team lead?" she asked, seeing a possible way out. If the sheikh asked for it, her career wouldn't be affected adversely. It was understood that some parts of the world did not deal as well with female geologists. "My superiors could arrange for my immediate replacement if that would make you more comfortable."

"Not at all. I am confident your work will be more than acceptable," Sheikh Hakim said smoothly.

Russell was staring at her like she'd offered to dance naked on the tabletop. Okay, so normally, she'd bristle and fight tooth and claw to avoid being replaced simply on the basis of gender, but these were special circumstances.

"It surprises me you would make the offer." Asad sounded just as disbelieving of her words. "I remember a woman who would not stand for the idea that men made better geologists than their female counterparts."

"I didn't say he would be a *better* geologist."

"Naturally not. You graduated at the top of your class, did you not?"

"I'm surprised you know that." But then it might well have been included in the information CC&B had supplied about her to Sheikh Hakim.

Asad shrugged again. "I kept up with you."

No, really, he hadn't. She'd never heard from him again after he left, though a mutual friend had told Iris when Asad had married a year after returning to his home. She'd spent the weekend crying off and on, for once Iris's studies unable to assuage the ache of loneliness and grief.

Then she'd buckled down, determined not to let anyone or anything stand in the way of the one dream she had left. She'd even continued her studies in Arabic, though until this assignment, she'd had no chance to use them in more than a few written translations and phone calls.

"I'm surprised your wife isn't with you," she said to change the topic and to remind herself forcibly why this man could not be allowed past her defenses.

No matter what the circumstances she would be forced to live in over the coming weeks.

And really? Where *was* the man's wife? What woman would prefer to stay at a Bedouin encampment when she could be visiting the local palace? And how did his wife feel about Asad promising protection and guidance to his former girlfriend?

But then, that at least, was an idiotic question. No way did the princess know anything about Iris.

Iris certainly hadn't known anything about Princess Badra when she'd been dating and sleeping with Asad.

Asad had known, though. He'd known he had no intention of spending his future with Iris. He'd known he planned to marry the virginal princess, not the American geology student who spent every night in his bed for ten months.

He'd seduced her anyway, treating Iris like his girl-friend when she was nothing but his mistress.

An old-fashioned word for an ugly, outdated position she would never have willingly taken. Or so she told herself.

The most painful truth of all, the one that had woken her in nighttime sweats more than once, was that even had she known he would never be hers, Iris was not sure she would have been able to walk away from what he offered her naive, love-struck, nineteen-year-old self.

"My wife died two years ago." Asad's voice pushed into Iris's raw thoughts.

She met his eyes in genuine shock and polite words tumbled out of her mouth in stark reaction. "I'm sorry."

Asad didn't reply, but looked back at her with an expression both predatory and implacable.

The room and people around them faded from her awareness for a frozen moment as she met his gaze, her body frozen in shock, her mind blank with reaction and her heart stuttering in horror.

A married Asad was bad enough, but a widower? The thought sent terror shaking through her not-so-mended heart.

* * *

The helicopter blades whirled overhead, making discussion within the bird impossible except over the shared radio pieces. Asad had his fill of public discourse the night before when all he'd wanted to do was drag Iris out of the dining room and take her somewhere they could be alone.

He could not pretend what he wanted to do was talk, either, though it was not entirely off the agenda.

It had taken considerable self-control to stop himself from going to visit her in her room, but he needed to follow his plan. A plan that had a better chance of success once she was living in his encampment, not minutes from the royal airfield at the palace.

The level of animosity in Iris's expression and voice when she wasn't doing her best to suppress it, surprised him. It had been six years since he'd returned home. Surely she was not still angry at the admittedly abrupt end to their association.

Had he to do it over again, he would have handled it differently. But when they'd been together, he hadn't realized she'd been thinking in terms of the future, either. He'd assumed from her actions and circumstances that she knew nothing they did together could be permanent. He hadn't counted on her Western viewpoint on feminine sexuality, or her ignorance of his status.

In his arrogance, he'd believed everyone knew he was a future sheikh. It was no secret after all. But Iris did not gossip, and she was a geology student who, he learned later, knew next to nothing about the students in her own discipline, much less the others that attended the large university with her.

When she'd told him she loved him, he'd taken it as his due. The usual response of a female in a sexual relationship with a man, but he hadn't believed she meant it.

He still wasn't sure he bought the idea of everlasting love, though his cousin's marriage to Catherine was something special. Even Asad could see that.

Nothing like his own marriage, which had been nothing more than a series of lies and subterfuge.

Still, he could have been kinder when he had to end their months-long affair. He realized that now.

He would never admit to anyone but himself that his harsh and immediate withdrawal had been the result of feelings he wasn't used to dealing with. He'd become more attached to Iris than he'd expected to. And much to his chagrin, had realized at the end of their time together, that she, more than anyone or anything else, had the possibility of undermining his carefully laid plans.

So, he had walked away. And stayed away.

And had forced his mind to shut down every time he thought of her until his ill-fated wedding night, when inevitable comparisons and conclusions had to be drawn. Conclusions that had destroyed what was left of his own naive beliefs about women and sex.

Iris hadn't been a virgin, but she'd been honest, loyal and surprisingly innocent. He'd believed Badra untouched, but that had been a lie of monumental proportions, as was so much about her. The woman who had considered herself too good for a Bedouin sheikh had traded on deceit and Asad had not even had a glimmer until their wedding night.

Even so, his anger at Badra had muted over time to be replaced with indifference. So that when she had died all he had felt was relief to be free of her, only marginally tinged by sadness for their daughter, who saw less of her mother than the Parisian clothiers Badra favored.

Once married, he'd been unable to keep thoughts of

Iris completely banked. Though that surprised him, he chalked it up to the fact that they had been even better friends than they were lovers. He'd kept up with her academic and work career, but had stayed away from her personally. He was not Badra. Asad did not cheat.

He did not understand this passionate fury barely contained in Iris, not after so much time. He slid a glance at her only to find her looking out the window of the helicopter, her eyes too unfocused to be seeing anything of real interest in the desert below.

Her body and attention turned from him, but he would change that. It had been six years. Two years since his wife's death. Enough time for all that he had planned. He would wait no longer.

The low mountains loomed much closer than at the palace when the helicopter made its descent for landing.

"Hey, where are the camels?" Russell asked as he climbed out of the helicopter right after the pilot.

Asad did not answer. He had not liked the way the field assistant referred to Iris proprietarily, and with such familiarity, the night before. Though he doubted very much that the two shared a relationship outside of work, Asad felt possessive of the friendship that had not been allowed to flourish by his marriage.

He offered his hand to help Iris alight. After a moment of inaction while she stared at his hand as if it were a snake set to strike, she very clearly gritted her teeth and then reached out to take it.

He smiled into her lovely sky-blue eyes, carefully blanked of emotion. "Welcome to the Bedouin of the twenty-first century."

Iris looked around them at the landing pad and the SUV parked on its edge. "I understand camels are not quite the mode of transport they once were." She met his gaze again and choked out a laugh which he enjoyed hearing very much. "But a Hummer?"

He shrugged. "What can I say? Our tribe is more affluent than most."

"Why is that?"

"My great-grandfather purchased land rights in three adjoining countries along our usual travel route so our tribe would always have a place to camp. At the time, political unrest dictated the move, but we rarely avail ourselves of that land for encampment anywhere but in Kadar."

"But the land in the other countries, it's making money for you?"

"It is." The once-beautiful landscape was marred by oil rigging that pounded away with a noise that others might learn to sleep through.

He never would. "Oil."

"Lucky you."

"Some might say so."

"I think pretty much everyone would say so."

He didn't reply, but turned to give instructions to the tribesmen waiting for them to move the geologists' luggage and equipment to the Hummer. Asad made sure Russell ended up in the other SUV for the drive.

The Sha'b Al'najid encampment was nothing like Iris expected. Erected in the shadows of the small mountain range in the southernmost part of Kadar, it truly looked like the "city of tents" Catherine had referred to.

"You must have high-producing wells."

"They are sufficient as a base for our needs."

"A base?"

"My grandfather invested intelligently if modestly on behalf of our people. I have continued that tradition, though perhaps not as modestly." Satisfaction glowed in Asad's dark gaze. "We continue to do what we are best at as a people, as well."

"What's that?" she asked, her curiosity stronger than her desire to avoid conversation with him.

"The Bedouin are known for their hospitality. Our tribe offers the opportunity to live the Bedouin life for tourists from the cities of Kadar and abroad. The Sha'b Al'najid still run trading caravans across the desert and for a sufficient fee, one may join in this venture, also."

"Like a Dude Ranch?" she asked in disbelief.

"I have never been to a Dude Ranch, but I believe the intent is similar. Others of my brethren tribes do this, as well. It provides our people the opportunity to continue with millennia of cultural and living traditions while others are afforded the opportunity to experience this unique way of life."

"You sound like a travel brochure."

"I have written more than one of them."

A grin sneaked up on her, despite her feelings toward him. "It can't be too traditional with Hummers instead of camels."

"We still have many camels, I assure you."

"Do you still move camp?"

"Twice a year, rather than seasonally, but yes."

"Do you stay in Kadar?"

"We do. This too is different, but preferable to other tribes who have settled permanently on lands granted by the government."

"I see." Though she wasn't really sure she did and was afraid he could hear it in the uncertainty of her tone.

"Within our encampment you will find modernizations mixed with traditions that are thousands of years old." And he was clearly proud of that fact.

"Are those electric cords?" she asked in shock as she noticed the thick black rubber-coated cords snaking through the sand.

"They are. We have a bank of solar panels strategically placed five hundred yards in that direction." He pointed away from the mountains to a spot that was no doubt ideal for sun exposure.

Incredible. "So, I can use my laptop?"

"It is better for you to charge your battery between uses. Our power is limited and certain measures must be taken, but there is even a television in the communal tent."

"I didn't know there was such a thing in a Bedouin encampment. I thought most of the socializing happened in individual homes." Or outside in the courtyard-like areas between the tents.

At least according to the research she'd done on Bedouin living back when she'd thought she'd had a reason to do so.

"The communal tent was created for the tourists to gather in groups, but my people have found they enjoy its use, as well."

"And its television."

"Some British and American programs are very popular." His shrug said some things must change, but others would remain the same. "I confess to a craving for *Law & Order* when I returned home six years ago."

They'd used to watch it together. He'd called the crime drama his weekly mindless entertainment. She never quite got that, but she'd suffered through the program's dark plots and emotional angst for the sake of spending that time with him.

"Do you still watch it?" he asked.

"No."

"It was never your favorite."

"No." Though she hadn't stopped watching until the series was canceled.

"Yet you watched it, for me."

This trip down memory lane was getting distinctly uncomfortable.

"I'll admit this is not what I expected." She waved her hand, indicating the encampment around her.

"You had expectations?"

"Naturally. It's a poor geologist who doesn't do her homework on the area she'll be surveying."

"But you had no idea you would be coming to a Bedouin encampment."

"You never know." It was not quite a lie, but not the admission he was looking for, either.

"This is true. Six years ago, neither of us would have suspected you would be here."

Actually, she had…right up until he'd broken up with her. She had no more interest in rehashing that particular bit of history than anything else about the months they'd been together. "You said some things are still traditional?"

"Many things."

She saw what he meant when they entered a huge tent toward the center of the encampment. A curtain bisected the area horizontally from the entrance. In the center, was a single overlapping panel embroidered with two giant peacocks, their feathers fanned out in a display of the beautiful jeweled tones the birds were known for.

The curtain created the public reception area the Bedouin homes were known for, but it was much larger she was sure than the average tent boasted. With no evidence of the famed television, Iris had to assume this wasn't the communal tent he'd mentioned earlier.

Rich Persian rugs covered the ground of the main area, but instead of chairs, there were luxurious pillows in silks, velvets and damasks with lots of gold, purple, teal and a dark sapphire blue. Low tables dotted the expansive area and while the outer walls were the typical woven black goat hair, inside the walls were covered in richly colored silks.

"Russell and I are staying here?" she asked with a sense of foreboding.

This was no normal Bedouin tent. Situated where it was in the compound and considering the luxury of the interior, she had no doubts who this particular dwelling belonged to. Sheikh Asad bin Hanif Al'najid.

"You are, yes. Russell will stay in the tent with your equipment."

"What is this tent, a harem, or something?" she asked in faint hope.

"This is my home."

CHAPTER THREE

"I'M NOT staying in your tent."

"It has been arranged. Your accommodations are behind that partition." He pointed at a blue silk hanging. "My late wife insisted on a nontraditional division of the women's area of the tent. So, you will have your own room rather than sharing the entire space with the other single women of my family."

"Other single women?" she asked faintly.

"My daughter and a distant cousin."

"I can't stay here with you."

"I assure you, you can."

"I'll share the tent with Russell."

Oh, Asad did not like that suggestion. Not at all. His expression went very dark very quickly. "You will not."

"But it makes the most sense." And might actually save her sanity, not to mention her heart.

"It is not acceptable."

"You and your cousin, Sheikh Hakim, have an affinity for that word," she grumbled, feeling like the Persian rug beneath her feet was actually quicksand.

"You will stay here." There was no give in Asad's voice or his posture.

"How is it better for me to stay here with you than to share a tent with Russell?"

"As I said, my daughter and cousin share this tent, as well, but so do my grandparents."

Her whirling brain latched onto the plural *grandparents* and she asked, "Your grandfather is still alive?"

"Of course."

"But you're sheikh."

"What did you think, I had to kill my predecessor to take over for him? It was much more prosaic. He retired and enjoys the increased freedom of his days like any other man who has well earned such."

"He retired?"

"Yes."

"That's just…"

According to what Iris had read, the concept of the next generation taking over the majority of sheikh responsibilities when the current holder of the office became very old was not completely unheard of. But to refer to it as *retirement?* It was just so, so…*modern.*

"The way of things." The words were spoken by an elderly woman carrying a tray with tea things on it as she entered through an opening in the blue silk partition.

Dressed in traditional Bedouin garb, the older woman's hair peeked from under a heavily embroidered and beaded sheer scarf that did not completely hide the long white tresses. Her face, though showing the wear of sun and years, was still beautiful, though paler than Asad and more Gallic in bone structure.

"Grandmother, may I present Miss Iris Carpenter." Asad bowed his head toward his grandmother while indicating Iris with his right hand. "Iris, my grandmother, the Lady bin Hanif."

"You will address me as Genevieve."

"Thank you. That is French, isn't it?" Iris asked, pretty sure the woman's accent was Gallic, as well.

"It is. Though my family has made its home in Switzerland for nearly two centuries. My husband found me when we were both attending university in Paris and convinced me to leave all I knew to share his life here among his Bedouin tribe." She smiled as she set the tea tray on one of the low tables. "I have never regretted it. The Sha'b Al'najid soon became my people."

"And Grandmother became the favorite lady to them in generations."

Iris smiled. "It's a pleasure to meet you, Genevieve."

"Come, sit." The older woman indicated the cushions on the floor with a flick of her elegant wrist. "It is always a pleasure to meet an old friend of my grandson."

About to deny the classification, Iris thought better of it. She suspected that the Lady bin Hanif was the type of woman who would demand an explanation.

"We knew each other only for a few short months at university," she said to downplay the relationship as much as possible.

Genevieve poured tea into fine china cups painted with Arabic design. "And yet those short months were particularly impacting for my grandson, I believe."

Iris turned to glare in shock at Asad. He'd told his grandparents about their affair? Heat crawled into her cheeks while her stomach rolled in humiliation.

Asad's eyes widened at her glare and then narrowed in what seemed like comprehension. He shook his head just slightly, as if saying he had not told them the intimate details of the friendship.

"Oh my, yes. Our boy, he spoke of hardly anyone

from his university days. But Iris, the budding geologist? We heard much of her academic and career ex-
ploits." Genevieve serenely sipped her tea. "His late
wife did not enjoy Asad's university reminiscences, I
think. She had attended only a year of finishing school
in Europe you see."

Completely flabbergasted by the idea that Asad had
kept track of her like he claimed, Iris could think of no
other response than to nod and sip her own tea. Hot,
very strong and almost equally sweet, it had a smoky
flavor something like Earl Grey and yet not. There was
almost a flavor of sage in the blend, as well.

"This is delicious. I can see why the Bedouin tea
is so famous."

"Yes. There is a knack to making it. You must brew
it over a wood fire, not on the hob."

Iris's gaze flicked to the silk divider. There was a
wood fire burning behind that, *inside* the goat hair
dwelling?

"Not to worry, the cooking fire is under the open
awning behind our tent," Asad said, showing more disconcerting proof that he could still read her all too well.

When they had been together, he had known her
better than anyone else, though she'd kept her secret
shame to herself and never admitted to him the extent
of her parents' indifference.

Genevieve smiled and reached out to pat Iris's arm.
"Do not worry. You will soon grow accustomed to our
ways."

"My favorite mentor always said that one of the
marks of a good field geologist is the ability to accli-
mate to different surroundings so nothing can get in
the way of accuracy in one's fieldwork."

"A wise man," Asad said, "was Professor Lester."

"How did you know I was talking about..." Iris let her voice trail off as Genevieve laughed softly.

"Oh, my grandson, he remembers everything, does he not?"

"Yes." Asad's eidetic memory was one of the reasons they'd had as much time together as they did.

When he had almost perfect recall of everything he heard, read and saw, the need to study for tests or reread information for papers was severely mitigated. He'd even helped Iris study for her own exams.

Genevieve's eyes glowed with pride as she looked at her grandson. "It makes him a very good sheikh and political advisor to my great-nephew, Hakim, ruler over all Kadar."

"You're one of Sheikh Hakim's official advisors?" Iris asked Asad, storing the information on their actual family relationship for future reference.

He merely nodded before taking a drink of tea.

But Genevieve was more forthcoming. "Of course, they are family. However, Asad has proven himself wise in the ways of our people and the modern world we must live in, as well. Hakim listens with a bent ear to our Asad. It was his idea, after all, to get your company to do the mineral survey and to request you be the on-site geologist."

Asad's jaw tautened, as if he was trying not to frown, but the look he gave his grandmother was tinged with something that looked very much like exasperation.

"You're the reason I wasn't given the option of refusing this assignment?" Iris demanded, catching on quickly even if her memory wasn't precisely eidetic.

Asad shrugged.

She opened her mouth to tell him that wasn't a good

enough answer. Not this time, but his grandmother forestalled Iris. "But why should you wish to?"

And Iris remembered where she was and why she was here, despite the helpless fury burning in her chest. "I have yet to do any survey work in the Middle East. Another geologist would have been a better choice."

"Nonsense. If Asad believes you will do the best job, then I am quite confident you will. Surely it is time you expanded your vita to include work in the Middle East."

Iris could not deny it. She would never be promoted to senior geologist while she lacked field experience in the Middle East, which was one of the points her boss had made when insisting Iris take this assignment.

That didn't make her feel any better about the revelation that Asad was responsible for getting Iris to Kadar. He was a man who always had an agenda. If she had only realized that when they'd been dating, she would not have been so sideswiped by the knowledge he was already practically engaged to the Princess Badra.

What was his plan now?

Iris had the awful feeling it had something to do with her. And since the only thing he'd wanted from her was her body, she didn't think she was too far outside the realm of probability to believe he had his sights set on renewing their affair.

For a short time anyway.

Why not? She'd fallen into his bed with barely a push back in the day. Practically a virgin, she'd still allowed him to make love...*or have sex rather*...with her on their first date. She'd been overwhelmed by her reaction to him and thought he felt the same. She knew better now, but wasn't entirely sure it would make any difference in the outcome.

"Where is your father?" she asked in a desperate attempt to change the subject and get her mind on a different pathway. Why hadn't *he* taken over the sheikh role?

And then she considered the possibility that the older man was deceased and wished she could bite the words back. Particularly after her similar faux pas the night before when asking about Asad's wife. It was too late, however, to do anything but hope she would not be given the same answer.

Thankfully, Asad did not look like he was remembering a traumatic loss. "He does not live with the tribe. He oversees our European interests from his home in Geneva."

"Your father lives in Switzerland?" Considering they clearly had family there, that was not entirely surprising. Still, it seemed odd that Asad would be sheikh to the nomadic Sha'b Al'najid while his father lived in one of the most sophisticated cities of Europe.

"As do his mother, sister and two brothers." Genevieve's tone did not sound altogether pleased by that fact.

Iris gave Asad a look in which she felt incapable of hiding her abject shock. "You have siblings?"

He had never mentioned it, but then he'd left a lot out of their discourse six years ago. So, the fact that none of them lived among the Bedouin tribe was even more surprising to her than their existence.

"It is so."

"But…"

Genevieve refilled the teacups without asking if Iris or Asad wanted more. Something about the set of her features told Iris this conversation was no easier on her than the earlier topic had been on Iris.

Asad leaned back on the cushion, looking like a

pasha and said, "You wonder why they do not live with the Sha'b Al'najid."

"If your parents live in Geneva, I suppose it's natural that your sister and brothers would, as well."

"They are all of an age to make their own decisions about how and where they live."

She didn't know what to say to that. She could understand that the Bedouin way of life might not work for everyone, but for all of them to turn their backs on thousands of years of tradition seemed wrong somehow.

"In order to gain permission to leave the tribe, my father had to allow my grandfather to raise me here as his own son to take over leadership of the tribe." Asad said it so casually, it took a moment for the import of his words to sink in. "It is why I am called bin Hanif instead of bin Marghub. Not that my father uses his tribal name. He goes by Jean Hanif."

In Western culture such a name similarity would show the family connection, but in Kadar, Asad not carrying his father's name was as good as disowning him. Though it sounded like the decision had been made for him.

"That's barbaric." Iris slapped her hand over her mouth, unable to believe she'd said that out loud, no matter how much she thought it.

She looked askance at the tea; was there something in there that she didn't know about?

Genevieve smiled reassuringly, clearly having taken no offense. "Jean found much about the Bedouin way of life to be barbaric. He never wished to return from our visits to Geneva to my family. He insisted on attending an American university and ended up married to a European like his father."

If they no longer lived among the tribe, Iris thought

that Western origin could be the only thing Asad's mother had in common with Genevieve.

"Celeste and Jean came here to live after their marriage, but neither were happy. Eventually, Jean told us that he had no desire to follow his father as sheikh to the Sha'b Al'najid. My husband could have named a cousin or nephew as his successor. It is how he became sheikh himself, but he saw the fire of the Bedouin burning brightly in our grandson and offered the alternative of us raising him here instead."

"How old were you when your parents left?" Iris asked.

"I was four."

And they had seen the Bedouin spirit burning bright in him? At such a young age? Iris supposed it was possible, but it was still barbaric. "How old were your siblings?"

"My sister was two. Mother was pregnant with my younger brother, as well."

"She did not want to give birth in the encampment." Genevieve shrugged, the movement exhibiting her Gallic ancestry. "All of her children were born in a Genevan hospital after Asad."

Despite their past, Iris could not help the rush of pity and understanding she felt for Asad in that moment. She knew exactly how it felt not to be necessary to one's parents.

Asad shook his head at her. "I know how you are thinking. Stop it. My parents did not abandon me. We continued to see one another often and I always had my grandparents. I had the Sha'b Al'najid. Doing things in such a fashion was necessary. My father did not want the less luxurious life of the Bedouin and my grandfather knew one day I would make an excellent sheikh."

No arrogance there. Not at all. She almost smiled. "It looks luxurious enough to me."

"We have satellite access to the internet for four hours in the afternoon only. We do not have modern kitchens, appliances or bathrooms."

She knew what he meant and shrugged. "I'm sure your facilities are better than what I have on most of my camping field assignments."

"No doubt." He smiled as though her words had pleased him, then the smile melted away as if it had never been. "What we have now is beyond what my father experienced in the encampment. Though when he and the others visit, they still find it abysmally rustic."

"All of them?"

"All but my youngest brother. He was born four years after they moved to Geneva." Asad's lips twisted wryly. "An unplanned blessing added to my parent's family. He has said he plans to make his home here once he finishes university."

"And your parents are okay with that?"

"Naturally. My father relies on the tribe's business investments for his income. He knows better than to reject our way of life completely." So, regardless of how unaffected Asad would like to appear regarding his father's rejection of his way of life, there was something there.

"He gave up his oldest son to the tribe," Genevieve chided. "Any parent would feel that was a sufficient sacrifice."

Iris begged to differ, but she wasn't about to say so out loud. Her parents would have happily given her up if it meant getting what they wanted. In fact, they had often made the trade-off of time with her for travel on their own. She'd never told Asad that she'd been sent to boarding school at age six, but then the fact had always shamed her.

She'd thought there was something wrong with her that her parents had preferred to have her live with them only on school vacations. And even then, they weren't always "at home" when she was.

"Perhaps," Asad replied to his grandmother, not looking particularly convinced. "I do not know how difficult the decision was for them. I know only that they made it, choosing life outside of the encampment rather than living here to raise me."

Genevieve clicked her tongue twice, as if gently chiding her grandson without saying anything overt.

"You never told me this." And Iris wasn't sure that hadn't been for the best.

She'd been head over heels in love with Asad, but how much worse it would have been for her if she'd believed they had this pain in common and allowed herself to identify with him on such a deep level?

"There was much we did not talk about."

"True. I didn't even know you were going to be sheikh one day." And he knew nothing of her childhood or her parents' supreme indifference. She'd never told him the story of how she'd lost her virginity. Asad was oh so right; there was *a lot* they'd never spoken of. "Looking back, I realize I should have guessed based on your bearing alone."

"I did not mean to hide that from you."

She believed him. He had been so certain she knew the score, she did not believe he'd meant to hide anything from her. For the first time in six years, she admitted to herself that they'd both been spectacularly wrong in reading the situation between them. Not just her.

That didn't do a thing to alleviate her current anger

with him for manipulating her into coming to Kadar, however.

Genevieve rose gracefully to her feet. "I will refresh the tea."

Iris went to stand, intent on helping, but the older woman placed a staying hand on her shoulder. "No. Another time, I will teach you to make tea the proper way. Now you must stay here and renew your acquaintance with my grandson. He has so looked forward to seeing you again."

Nonplussed, Iris could do nothing but nod with as much graciousness as she could muster. She didn't think it would do her company's relationship with Kadar a good turn if Iris admitted she would rather renew the acquaintance of the rattlesnake she'd met on her last field survey than Asad's.

Asad waited until his grandmother had gone to say, "I never lied to you. I thought you knew I was meant to be a sheikh."

"I heard you the first time." She glared at him, her current anger sufficient to fuel the nasty look, their past notwithstanding.

"And?"

What? Was he expecting her to congratulate him or something?

"Do you believe me?" he asked with a tinge of frustration in his usually urbane tones.

"Yes."

"Then why the look when grandmother left us to talk?"

Really? He could not be that dense. "I guess an eidetic memory does not equate to people smarts."

His eyes narrowed in affront at her sarcasm. "You have changed."

"Yes." She was no naive idiot anymore. "But seriously? How could you think knowing you would be a sheikh one day would have made a difference to me back then? I wouldn't have been any more prepared to be dumped like I was."

"I did not dump you."

What happened to that famed honesty of his? "Excuse me, *you did*."

"I had obligations, a plan for my life I could not abandon."

"You didn't want to abandon it. You didn't leave me out of duty—you left because you *never* wanted me for a lifetime. I was just stupid enough to believe you did. That's all." And equally painful, she'd lost her best friend.

"I am sorry."

He had said *that* six years ago too, with pity in his eyes. But not regret. If there was regret there now, she wouldn't let herself see it.

"It's in the past."

"Yet I still see pain in your eyes when you talk about it."

She couldn't deny it, but she sure wasn't going to admit to it, either. She'd had all the pity she could stand from this man when she'd been that foolishly naive nineteen-year-old. Besides, she had something much more recent to deal with.

"I can't believe you engineered me coming to Kadar." She made zero effort to hide how much knowledge of his manipulation infuriated her.

He looked shocked by her anger. "I was doing you a good turn, making up for my abrupt departure from your life, if you will."

"You have absolutely got to be kidding me. You

think being forced to work in close proximity to you is in some way a good thing?"

"I am no monster. You used to enjoy my company very much, and I do not just mean in the bedroom."

"We were friends. We aren't anymore!" She swallowed her next words and fought for control of her vocal cords. The last thing she wanted was for Genevieve to return to Iris shouting at the man she was beginning to realize was more dense than metamorphic rock.

"We could be again."

"Why?" Why would he want to be?

"I missed you. You missed me."

And to him, it was that simple. Never mind the fact she'd been so totally in love with him that she'd felt like her heart had been ripped from her chest when he left. "You could have just called."

"You needed the Middle East experience to move forward with your career."

"Just how close tabs have you been keeping?" she demanded.

"Close enough."

"So, you thought you'd do me a favor?" Why did she think it hadn't all been altruism on his part? Oh, yes, because she no longer trusted him and never would again. "Didn't it occur to you that not coming to the Middle East had been my decision?"

"No."

She dropped her head in her hands and groaned, her fury losing its heat. The man just had no clue, none whatsoever.

And there was no point in continuing this discussion. He was never going to get it, but he wasn't going to drop the subject unless she did.

So she observed, "You said you share this tent with your family."

"I do."

"Where is everyone else?" Were the tent walls so thick, they would mask the sounds of a child?

It was surprisingly quiet, no sounds from outside filtering through, nor from any other part of the tent.

"My grandfather spends this time each day with the other old men, drinking coffee and telling stories. No doubt he would have stayed to meet your arrival, but my grandmother knows how to get her way and she wanted to meet you first," Asad revealed in a fond tone.

"Where is your daughter? In school?" Iris guessed.

He shook his head. "She will be playing with other small children under the watchful eye of my cousin."

Since, presumably, if his grandparents had more children than Asad's father, the barbaric bargain would not have been made, he didn't mean *cousin* literally, but referred to a female relative. "She's not old enough for school?"

"We do not run a school precisely, though the concept is similar. We train our children in every aspect of life, not merely to read, write and cipher, though we do not neglect their book learning. Some will want to attend university one day." He reached out as if to touch Iris and let his hand fall, an unreadable expression in his dark eyes. "But you are right, my daughter is too young for any formalized training."

"Does your grandmother have someone to help her with…" She let her voice trail off, not knowing the child's name.

"Nawar. My daughter's name is Nawar and she is four. My grandmother and cousin help me with Nawar, but she is *my daughter*."

"That is a commendable attitude to take," she grudgingly admitted. "But I would have thought that since you're the sheikh, you'd be too busy for full-time parenting."

"Is it so unusual for a father to have a career? I do not think so. I spend as much time with Nawar as possible."

Once again, Iris believed him, but wished she didn't. It would be a lot easier on her if she could simply see him as a complete and utter bastard. Instead, he made himself all too human. If they did not have the shared past they did, she would not only respect him, but she might even like him, as well.

Something she simply could not afford to let herself do.

CHAPTER FOUR

"I WOULD be more comfortable staying in another tent." Iris knew this was her only chance to argue her viewpoint and she should not have wasted time discussing their past.

"Would you really?"

"Yes."

"You wish to stay with strangers?" he asked in a tone that said he knew she would not.

"That's not what I meant."

"But that is the only other option."

"Well then, maybe it would be best." As much as she hated the idea, it was better than living in his home.

"No."

Typical Asad-like response. He didn't bother to justify, or excuse; he simply denied.

"You've gotten even bossier since university," she accused him.

Though back then, his bossiness had not bothered her. He'd convinced her to try things she never would have otherwise, like the ballroom dancing class they'd taken together a month after they'd met, or attending parties she wouldn't have been invited to on her own and learning to dance to modern music amidst a group of her peers.

She'd suppressed so many of the good memories from their time together and now they were slipping their leash in her mind.

He did not look particularly bothered by her indictment. "Perhaps."

"There is no perhaps about it."

"And you are surprised? I am a sheikh, Iris. Bossiness is in the job description." He sounded far too amused for her liking.

"Asad, you've got to be reasonable."

"I assure you, I am eminently reasonable."

"You're stubborn as a goat."

"Are goats so stubborn then?"

"You know they are."

"I would know this how?" he asked in an odd tone.

She rolled her eyes. "Because everybody does."

He nodded, tension seeming to leave his shoulders, though she had no clue what had caused it. "You will stay here."

"You're a CD with a skip in it on this."

"First a goat, now broken sound equipment. What will you liken me to next?"

"You're changing the subject."

"There is nothing further to discuss in it."

She opened her mouth to tell him just how much more there was to discuss when a flurry at the door covering caught Iris's attention. A second later a small girl with long black hair came rushing into the tent and threw herself at Asad's legs. "Papa!"

He leaned down and picked her up, giving her a warm hug and kiss on her cheek. "My little jewel, have you had a good morning?"

Other than the coloring, Iris did not see the family

resemblance. The little girl must take after her mother. The observation made Iris's heart twinge.

"I missed you, Papa, so much. I even cried."

"Did you?"

She nodded solemnly. "Grandmother said I needed to be strong, but I did not want to be strong. Why didn't you take me with you, Papa?"

Asad winced as if regretting his decision to leave his daughter behind. "I should have."

"Yes. I like playing at the palace with my cousins."

"I know you do."

"Next time, I must go."

"I will consider it."

"Papa!"

"Stop, you are being very rude. There is someone here for you to meet and you have spent all this time haranguing me."

Watching the two together caused that same delight tinged with pain she felt around Catherine and Sheikh Hakim. It was so clear that Asad loved his daughter and that pleased Iris because it meant she had not been entirely wrong about this man six years ago. She'd thought he would make a wonderful father and she'd been right, but knowing he'd had his child with another woman sent salt into old wounds.

"Oh, I am sorry." The little girl looked around and locked gazes with Iris, her dark eyes widening. "Who are you?"

"Nawar," Genevieve chided, coming back into the room with a laden tray the cousin jumped forward to relieve her of.

It was clear from the extra cups and amount of food that Genevieve had expected the child's return with her minder, a woman about fifteen years Asad's senior with soft brown eyes.

The little girl looked properly chastised, her expression going contrite. "I did not mean to offend." She put out her little hand from her position in her father's arms. "I am Nawar bin Asad Al'najid."

She sounded just like a miniature grown-up and Iris was charmed. She took the little girl's hand and shook gently. "My name is Iris Carpenter. It is a pleasure to meet you, Miss Bin'asad."

"Thank you. Why do you call me Miss Bin'asad?"

"Iris is being polite," Asad answered before Iris could.

"Oh. But I want her to call me Nawar. It is my name."

Iris had spent very little time around small children, but she thought Nawar must be exceptional. "I will be honored to call you Nawar and you may call me Iris."

"Really?" the girl asked. She looked to her grandmother. "It is all right?"

"If she gives you permission to do so, yes," the older woman said with firm certainty.

"Iris is a pretty name," Nawar offered.

"Thank you. It is my mother's favorite flower." She'd decided her mother chose the name so she would not forget it as easily as she and Iris's father forgot their only child. "Nawar is lovely, as well. Do you know what it means?"

"It means flower. Papa named me."

Iris did not know why Asad had named his daughter rather than his wife doing so; perhaps it was a Bedouin tradition, though that sounded rather odd considering the other cultural norms she had read about among his nomadic people.

It was those norms that made it possible for Iris to

stay in Asad's familial tent, but would have made it impossible if he did not live with his grandparents. She could wish he'd broken more cultural norms and moved into his own dwelling, so she didn't have to.

"Your papa is very good at naming little girls, I think."

"I do, too." Nawar smiled shyly. "What is haranguing? Do you know?"

Asad huffed something that could have been a laugh.

Iris stifled her own humor and answered, "It's like nagging."

Nawar turned her head to glare at her father. "I don't nag, Papa."

"Sometimes, little jewel, you do."

The little girl sniffed and it was all Iris could do not to burst out laughing. An urge Iris surprisingly felt several times over the next hour, while sharing more tea and refreshments with Asad's family. His grandfather joined them not long after Nawar had arrived, evincing the same pleasure in Iris's presence as Genevieve had done.

Iris expected Russell to arrive any minute, but the minutes ticked by and he didn't. When she asked, Iris was told he had been given a tour of the encampment by one of Asad's tourist liaisons.

She couldn't quite suppress her disappointment at the news. "Oh, I would have liked to have joined him."

"I am glad to hear you say so. I planned to give you a tour later," Asad said with satisfaction.

Iris just stopped herself from gaping and said, "I wouldn't want to take up more of your valuable time as sheikh."

The man was relentless. He wanted to renew their friendship and he would make that happen. One way or another. Maybe he did regret the way things had happened between them and this was his attempt at making up for it, but still…she hadn't imagined that predatory look in his eyes, either.

He probably saw nothing wrong with adding sex to their friendship. He'd done it once before, after all.

"Nonsense, you are a guest in our home. Asad would not dream of neglecting you while you are here," his grandfather said with finality.

Iris thought she knew where the younger sheikh had gotten his arrogance, and it wasn't from a stranger. But the older man's point about the Bedouin tradition of hospitality could not be ignored, either. From what she had read, it was not a matter of pride, but one of honor.

And honor could not be dismissed.

"May I go, Papa?" Nawar asked.

Iris smiled at the little girl in encouragement, but Asad shook his head. "You will be napping, I am afraid."

"I'm not tired." Nawar negated the words almost instantly by rubbing her eye with her small fist. "I want to go."

Her father pulled Nawar into his lap and kissed her temple. "You need your rest, but be assured Iris will still be here when you wake and for many days after. Won't you, Iris?"

Iris could do nothing but agree. Asad and his cousin had maneuvered her neatly into a situation she saw no way out of without severe damage to her career.

Genevieve showed Iris to her room while Asad put Nawar down for a nap.

"It's beautiful. Thank you." Both private and luxurious, the apartment was larger than she'd expected.

The bed was ground level and a single, though. Covered in rich silks a deep teal color she'd always loved, it looked very comfortable nonetheless. Graced with fluffy pillows Iris was certain just from looking at them were of the finest down, the bed tempted her to simply sink down and take her own afternoon nap.

Genevieve nodded and smiled. "Asad had someone come in and change the decor to better fit in with the rest of our home after Badra's death. During their brief marriage, moving this room alone was almost as big of a job as moving the entire encampment."

"I'm...this used to be the princess's room?" Iris asked faintly, relieved that while still luxurious, it wasn't anywhere near as ostentatious as Genevieve implied it had once been.

Though the fact the princess had called it her own would explain the amount of space dedicated to it in a Bedouin tent, regardless of the fact the sheikh's dwelling was probably one of the largest in the encampment.

"Oh, yes." Genevieve indicated the fabric wall the bed butted up against. "Asad's room is just on the other side."

"But isn't that...I mean, aren't the male and female quarters separated?"

"In a traditional tent, yes, but I must admit to making some changes in our home when I married Hanif and Badra made even more. While the receiving room is traditional, the way we divide what used to be considered the women's space is quite different."

"I see." Though honestly, Iris felt very much in the dark.

"Hakim and I have the room at the end, beyond the interior kitchen. Fadwa and Nawar share the room between it and us. And you are correct, in the Bedouin culture, usually a single woman would stay in that room with them, but Asad has decreed you would be more comfortable in Badra's old lodgings."

The older woman waited as if expecting Iris to say something, so she said, "Um…I'm sure he's right."

Neither woman commented on the fact that the sheikh and his wife had not shared sleeping quarters. But Iris couldn't help speculating on the why of it. Had the virtuous Badra found the wedding bed too onerous?

Unimaginable. How could any woman not fall under the sensual spell Asad created in the bedroom? When they were together, she'd craved his touch with an intensity that had shamed her after the breakup. At the time though, she'd been enthralled by the beauty and passion of their lovemaking.

It was simply unfathomable to her that another woman would be indifferent to Asad's sexual prowess.

Needing to redirect her thoughts, Iris reached out to touch the brass pitcher beside a matching basin on top of the single chest of drawers. "This is lovely."

Decorated with an intricate design surrounding a proud peacock, it was polished to a bright sheen.

"The water in the pitcher is clean. You may drink it, or use it to wash," Genevieve said. "Someone will come to dispose of the water in the basin for you. It will be used to water my garden in the back, so it is important you only use the soap provided."

Iris picked up the bar of handmade soap and sniffed. The fragrance of jasmine mixed with sage. "I'll be happy to. This is wonderful."

"I am glad you think so." Something in her tone said that perhaps the perfect princess, Badra, had not. "We make it here in the encampment."

Iris noted that her case was beside the chest, but she

hadn't seen anyone come in while they were visiting over tea. "Is there another entrance to the tent?"

Genevieve nodded with a warm smile. "Through the kitchen. I will show you the rest of our humble home, if you would like?"

"Oh, yes, please."

The tent dwelling was anything but humble, the private compartments all endowed with the same level of luxury as Iris's room, if not a plethora of furniture that might make their twice-a-year resettlement difficult. Or at least, Iris assumed Nawar and Fadwa's was, but she had been unable to see for herself as the child was settling into her nap.

One thing she did note was that the single women's quarters that housed Asad's daughter and distant cousin were actually smaller than the apartment Badra had commandeered for her own use and that Iris would now use.

When she said as much to Genevieve, the other woman shrugged. "Perhaps when Asad marries again, his wife will reapportion the sleeping quarters again. So long as she does not attempt to change my and Hanif's room, I will be content."

"Is he thinking of remarrying then?" The thought of Asad taking another wife sent a shard of pain that absolutely should not be possible straight through Iris's heart.

"But naturally. Though he has not set his sights on any woman in particular." Genevieve led the way through the inner kitchen and outside. "Enough time has passed since Badra's death though, I think."

"How did she die?"

"In a plane crash with her lover," Asad said with brutal starkness from behind Iris.

His arrival taking her by surprise, she jumped and spun to see him standing with an old familiar arrogance, but an only recently familiar harsh cast to his features.

Genevieve tutted at her grandson. "Really, Asad, you needn't announce it in such a manner."

"You think I should dress it up? Pretend she was simply vacationing with friends as the papers reported?"

"For the sake of your daughter, yes, I do."

Asad inclined his head. In agreement? Perhaps, but the man wasn't giving anything away with his expression.

"What do you think of my home?" he asked, dismissing the topic of his unfaithful wife in a way that shocked Iris.

The Asad she had known at university would never have been so pragmatic about such a betrayal.

Forcing her own mind to make the ruthless mental adjustment of topics, she said rather faintly, "It's fantastic."

"You like your room?" he asked, the stern lines of his face relaxing somewhat.

She tried to keep the hesitation she was feeling from her tone. "Yes."

"But?"

"I didn't say anything."

"Didn't you?" Asad's tone was borderline cutting.

"It's just that, well…it's kind of big for just me, isn't it? I mean, it's gorgeous, but I could set my lab up in the room and still have plenty of room to spare." She felt guilty about that fact, though she wasn't sure why.

Not to mention, it was right next to Asad's room. That in itself was enough to cause immeasurable anxiety and probably sleeplessness on her part.

One of his now rare but gorgeous smiles transformed Asad's features. "That will not be necessary. You and your coworker have already been assigned quarters for your tests."

"Thank you." What else could she say?

"I will do all that I can to make your stay here a pleasant one." The words were right, but the look that accompanied them sent an atavistic shiver down Iris's spine.

She turned to take in the charming courtyard created by the surrounding tents. Jasmine and herbs in pots decorated with bright mosaics made the space seem anything but desert austere. Despite the heat, other women cooked over open campfires, their curious gazes sliding between their sheikh's guest and the watch they kept over children playing in the communal area.

"I had read that the tents are grouped by family ties. Is that true here among the Sha'b Al'najid?" Iris asked.

"It is," Asad answered while his grandmother conferred with the woman cooking what Iris assumed was to be *their* dinner. "The dwellings around us are those of the family closest to my grandfather's predecessor. Had my grandparents had more children, it would be their tents that occupied these spots around the sheikh's home."

It must have been a great disappointment to the elder couple to have only had one child, but Iris kept her lips clamped over the much too personal thought.

"Come." Asad took Iris's hand and placed it on his arm. "I will show you the rest of our city of tents."

"Do you have the time, really?" she asked, trying to tug her hand away to no avail.

His other hand held it implacably in place and his

dark gaze told her he wasn't about to let go. "I have made time. The law of hospitality is very important among the Bedouin. Not to show you proper consideration as a guest in my home would be unacceptable."

"There's that word again."

A tiny lift at the corner of Asad's lips could have been a smile of amusement, but he was such a serious man now. She could not be sure.

"The way of life among my people is thousands of years old. Some things are considered absolute."

"Like hospitality," she guessed.

"Yes."

"But your home is not as traditional as it appears."

"No."

"You are not afraid of change."

"I am not, though I do not seek it for its own sake."

"You want to keep the Bedouin way of life viable coming into the next generations."

"You understand me well." His hand tightened on hers. "You always did."

"No." If she'd really understood him six years ago, she never would have deceived herself into believing what they had was permanent.

"Perhaps you understood me better than I did myself."

"Oh, no. We are not going there." She tried to yank her hand away again.

But he held on. "Be at peace, *aziz.* We will shelve the discussion of our past friendship for now."

If only he was simply talking about friendship. She'd become friends with Russell since he started his internship, but Iris was under no illusions. When he returned to university, if they never spoke again, she would not be devastated.

Not like after she'd lost Asad.

When she'd believed they were far more than friends who had sex. "No. Don't. You don't mean that word. Don't ever use it with me again. I don't care if you see it as a casual endearment, I do not...I didn't back then and it hurt more than you'll ever understand to learn it meant less than nothing to you."

"What?" He'd stopped with her, his tone filled with genuine incomprehension. "What has you so agitated?"

He really didn't know and that said it all, didn't it?

"*Aziz.* You will not call me that. Do you understand me? If you do it again, I will leave...I promise you." She knew she didn't sound superbly rational, or even altogether coherent, but she wasn't backing down on this.

Shock and disbelief crossed his face before the sheikh mask fell again. "You would compromise your career over a single word?"

"Yes." And she meant it. She'd tolerate a lot, but not that.

Not ever again. That single word embodied every aspect of pain that had shredded her heart six years ago. It meant *beloved,* but he didn't mean it that way. He'd never once told her he loved her, but every time he called her *aziz,* she'd believed that was his way of doing so.

She'd been so incredibly wrong, but darn it—the word had only one translation that she knew of. Only Asad used the word as flippantly empty as a rapper calling his female flavor of the week "baby."

Iris and Asad stood in the middle of a walkway between tents, others walking by them, but no one stopped to converse with their sheikh. It was as if they could sense the monumental emotional explosion pressing against the surface of normality she'd been striving for since seeing him at the bottom of the stairs the night before.

"You do not wish me to call you *aziz,* but surely—"

"No. Promise me, or I'm going to pack my things up right now."

"Your company would not be pleased."

"They'll probably fire me."

"And yet, you would leave Kadar anyway." The confusion in his tone hurt as much as his casual use of the word a moment before.

"Yes." She didn't care if he understood; she only wanted his compliance. "Are we in agreement?"

After several seconds of charged silence he said, "I will not use the endearment unless you give me leave to do so."

"It will never happen." That was one thing she was sure of.

"We shall see."

"Asad—"

"No. We have had enough emotional turmoil this day. I will show you my desert home and you will fall in love with the Sha'b Al'najid just as so many have before you."

And then leaving them would break her heart, but that seemed par for the course with this man for her.

She could do nothing but nod. "All right."

He showed her the communal tent he was so proud of. Even in the middle of the day, it was busy with people, some watching a tennis match on the large projector screen while others occupied themselves more traditionally with a game as old as their lifestyle played with pebbles or seeds.

"So, this is where the tourists congregate?" she

asked, doing her best to ignore the effect his nearness had on her body.

After six years and a broken heart, no less. It wasn't fair. Not one little bit. But he was right; they'd had enough emotional upheaval today and she wasn't going to invite more by letting herself get lost in her reaction to him.

"Usually, but we have no guests at present."

"Why not?"

"The most recent group left and the next does not arrive for a few days."

"You timed it, didn't you?" She didn't know why or even how he could have maneuvered her arrival to fit his liking, but she knew he had.

He didn't even bother to shrug, just gave her a look that she had no hope of reading and wasn't sure she'd want to if she could.

CHAPTER FIVE

By the time they had seen a good deal of the encampment, Iris's head was spinning with images and thoughts.

She'd met women who spent their days weaving amazing rugs and fabrics, others who beaded jewelry, and some even making the soap Genevieve preferred. A much smellier occupation than the fragrant bar Iris had sniffed earlier might have implied.

She saw much she expected to, traditional Bedouins doing traditional things and she really loved it. Few experiences could live up to imagination, but life here among the Sha'b Al'najid? It absolutely did.

"But where are the herds?" she asked, as they approached a tent that stood off by itself.

It was near his home and where they had started and she knew they were close to the end of the tour. Inexplicably, she was not ready for her time with him to be over. She tried to convince herself that was because she wanted to know more about the Bedouin, but she'd never been very good at lying to herself.

Sheikh Asad bin Hanif Al'najid was every bit as fascinating to her as he had been when he was simply Asad Hanif. If she were honest with herself, he was even more so. She needed to get to work quickly and get her mind occupied elsewhere.

"Herds?" he asked, his tone curiously flat after the animation with which he'd described his home over the past two hours.

"The goats and things. I'd always read that Bedouins kept flocks." Only the encampment had been surprisingly bereft of animals, except, surprisingly, some peacocks and peahens wandering between the tents, which she assumed they kept as a curiosity for the tourists.

From what she could tell, the birds had free rein of the encampment and were quite friendly. However, they'd been the only evidence of animals she'd seen. Unless others were kept in the courtyards, but there hadn't been any in the one behind his tent.

"And you thought all Bedouins were goatherds?" he asked with a stark tension she did not understand.

"Don't be ridiculous—no more than I think everyone living in the Midwest is a farmer, but isn't herding part of the traditional Bedouin way of life?" Not only would it not make sense for the Sha'b Al'najid to get their meat and fleece elsewhere, considering how independent a people she'd already witnessed they were, but wouldn't the tourists expect it?

"We do keep herds, rather a lot of them in fact, but they are grazed in the foothills. If they were not, the stench might be too much for our guests."

"That makes sense." Though somehow, she wasn't sure how she felt about them pushing a traditional part of their lifestyle into the outskirts.

He lifted a sardonic brow. "I'm glad you think so."

"I didn't mean to offend you." Wasn't even sure how she had done so.

Asad shook his head. "You did not. It was an old argument I had with Badra. That is all."

Surprised again by his candid comment about his

deceased wife, Iris nevertheless asked, "Did she think it wrong to cater so carefully to the tourist's preferences?"

Asad's laughter sounded more like glass breaking. "Not at all. Quite the opposite, in fact. She could not stand the smell and would have preferred we got rid of the herds altogether."

He'd already alluded to the fact his wife had not been faithful—an eventuality Iris simply could not comprehend. What woman would want another man when she had Asad in her bed? But this latest revelation pointed to only one conclusion: the perfect princess had been a perfect idiot.

Because the woman would have to be absolutely brainless not to realize how foolish it would be to give up the herds of a Bedouin tribe.

"Marrying the virginal princess did not turn out to be all it was cracked up to be, I guess."

"If that odd English idiom means it was not what I expected it to be, you are correct. Does that please you?" he asked darkly.

"You probably won't believe me, but no. Losing what I thought I had with you hurt more than I believed anything ever could, but I never wished you ill." Her own honesty surprised her a little, but with only a couple of glaring exceptions, she'd always found it far too easy to reveal her deepest thoughts and emotions to Asad.

Perhaps because in the past, he'd proven himself a worthy and safe confidant. It was hard to change that viewpoint despite the pain he'd put her through, maybe because he'd walked away and she hadn't had a chance to shore up her defenses against him in person.

Whenever she'd revealed a fear or disappointment in the past, he did his best to alleviate it. She'd told him she was worried about passing a difficult class and though it was not in his discipline, he'd helped her study and even write one of her papers. She'd admitted to feeling awkward in the way her body moved and he'd talked her into ballroom dancing lessons.

Asad stopped before they entered the strangely isolated tent and looked down at her. "You are a very different sort of woman, little flower."

He'd used to call her that, too, a play on her name that was just silly enough to be endearing. Somehow, his using it again didn't hurt with nearly the pain the betraying *aziz* had done.

"I don't think so. When you love someone, you want them to be happy. Even when it's not with you." That truth had sustained her through some of the darkest nights of her soul.

He jolted as if she'd hit him with a cattle prod. "You love me?"

"I *loved* you," she emphasized.

"And that prevented you from hating me?" he asked in a curious tone. "Even though you considered my leaving a betrayal."

"It was a betrayal of my love. But no, I don't hate you."

She never had, even in her darkest moments of pain. A love as deep as the one she felt for him simply had not allowed for that emotion, no matter how devastated she'd been.

He went as if to touch her face, but then let his hand drop after a quick glance around. They were not alone, though no one was close enough to hear the subject of their conversation. It would not do for him to be seen taking such liberties with a single woman, even one from the West.

The tribe might be part of the small percentage of

Bedouins that had not converted to Islam in the seventh century, but that did not mean that such behavior would be any more culturally acceptable in this place.

"Your love for me was true," he said as if just realizing that.

"And you really *didn't* love me. Life is peppered with little inconsistencies like that," she said with a wry twist to her lips.

She was really proud of the insouciance of her tone and stance. Maybe seeing him again had been for the best. Perhaps once this assignment was over, Iris would be able to move forward with her life…and maybe even fall in love with someone who would return her feelings.

Though trusting someone else with her heart was not something she was sure she ever wanted to do again.

"So, what is this place?" she asked, indicating the isolated tent.

"Let me show you," he said as he led her inside.

She gasped out in shock as they passed under the heavy tent flap that operated as the door.

The interior of this particular structure was nothing like the others. An undeniably modern office, either side of the main area, was taken up by two desks facing each other, all manned by people clearly at work. In the center, there was even a secretary/receptionist speaking into a headset while typing at a laptop on her desk.

No one sat on cushions on the floor, like in other Bedouin tents. In fact, there were no cushions. They all used leather office chairs and the receptionist had a small grouping of armchairs covered in Turkish damask in front of her desk. The potted plants to either side of her desk looked real and native to the desert, and the desks were made from dark wood with a definite Middle Eastern vibe, but other than that, this room could pass for any office in corporate America or Europe.

The receptionist looked up at their entrance, nodded at Asad in acknowledgment and gave a small smile to Iris, but then went back to her phone conversation. He didn't seem bothered by the lack of formal greeting.

"What is this? Command central?" Iris asked.

That surprised a laugh out of Asad that sounded quite genuine and she had to stifle her own grin in response.

"I suppose you could call it that. Come." He led her through the busy room to a curtain similar to that in any other Bedouin tent, except this one had an arched opening cut out in the center that led to a hall.

On the right side, they could see through the opening to a room with a bevy of monitors on one wall. Two men and a woman watched, taking notes and calling out observations to each other, or speaking into headsets as they did so.

"This is where we monitor our caravans, the encampment and other business interests."

The room to the left proved to be Asad's office. She had no doubts as to who it belonged as soon as they entered. For one thing, it had the equivalent of a door, heavy fabric that fell into place cutting off the sound of the others working within the tent office.

For another, the space was decorated with dark wood and rich colors similar to those in his home. And it simply *felt* like it belonged to Asad.

"I thought Bedouin sheikhs conducted business over the campfire," she remarked, still a little flabbergasted by this modern hive of corporate activity in the midst of a Bedouin camp.

"We are not so primitive, though I still settle most disputes among our people over a traditional cup of tea."

"That's good to know. I wouldn't want to think you'd abandoned your old ways completely."

"I have not abandoned them at all. I've simply made them work in a modern age as you guessed earlier."

"You're a very wise man." She didn't mind giving the compliment. It was well deserved.

But that was all he was getting from her. No matter how heated his dark gaze had gotten since their arrival in the private room. She didn't miss the fact that there was a low divan that could easily be used for sleeping when he did not return home at night.

"You're just as much of a workaholic here as you were at university, aren't you?" She'd bet even more so.

Asad shrugged. "I have the welfare of many people on my shoulders. It does not make for long nights of sleep."

"If I remember right, you weren't fond of sleeping as a student, either."

"But for entirely different reasons." The look he gave her could have melted iron.

But she wasn't going to let it melt her heart. "Get that look off your face. I'm here to do a geological survey for Sheik Hakim, nothing more. And we were enjoying this tour. Don't ruin it."

"I assure you, that is not my intention." He moved closer and being smarter than she had been six years ago, she backed up.

Only, when her thighs hit his desk, she knew she was trapped. She put her hands up. "Stop. What happened to having enough emotional drama for one day?"

"I have no intention of indulging in drama. I have something else entirely in mind."

She shook her head, doing her best to look firm while her body yearned for his touch with a reawakened and near-terrifying passion. "We aren't doing this."

"Are you certain?" he asked, his muscular legs coming to a stop only a breath of air away from hers.

"I am. I mean it, Asad. I'm not here for a dalliance. I'm here to work."

"A dalliance." He reached up and caressed the outer shell of her ear exposed by her hair pulled back in a ponytail. "An interesting and strangely old-fashioned word for a modern-day geologist."

"Maybe I'm a little old-fashioned."

"The woman who allowed me entrance to her body on our first date? One who had others before me? I think not."

She shoved at him, hard, his words a better deterrent to her giving in than anything she could have come up with. "You don't know anything about me."

He actually stumbled back a step; maybe in surprise at the strength of her attack. He might be playing, but she wasn't. She slid away from him quickly, stopping only when she was near the door and could make an instant escape if necessary.

The arrogant assurance in his stance and demeanor did not change at all. "I think I know some things about you very well."

"You knew me six years ago. Things change. People change." Please God, let her have changed enough.

"If that were so, you would not be afraid of what you would reveal with my nearness."

Oh, he had more nerve than a snake oil salesman and was just as trustworthy to her heart. She had to remember that. "Maybe I simply don't enjoy being sexually harassed on the job."

"You do not work for me."

"I work for your cousin."

"But not for me. You and I both know your job with Hakim in no way relies on what happens between us."

"Or doesn't happen?" she taunted.

But he nodded decisively. "Or doesn't happen. You want me, Iris. I can see it in the flutter of your pulse here," he pointed to his own neck. "And the way you lose your breath when I am near."

She slapped her hand over her neck, as if she could hide the evidence, but knew he was right. "I am not controlled by the urges of my body."

"So, you admit you desire me? I will take that as a start."

"You're a fantastic lover, Asad, but you're lousy odds for a relationship and I'm not interested in a brief sexual encounter."

His nostrils flared, like they used to when he was particularly turned on. "When we make love, it will be anything but brief."

"And anything but love." Regardless of the corresponding heat pooling in her womb. "It's not going to happen."

"You are lying to yourself."

"You go right on believing that and while you are at it, leave me alone." She fled from the office and then the tent, heading back into the encampment toward the one Asad had pointed out earlier that housed both Russell and their equipment.

Asad had refused to stop and let her explore then, saying there would be plenty of time for her to spend in that particular dwelling. She intended to make that true.

She didn't care if her hasty exit and walk through the city of tents was considered dignified. She didn't have to be a general to know when all-out retreat was called for.

She was only surprised when Asad did not pursue her, but then perhaps he was more aware of his own dignity than she was of hers.

Russell evinced no surprise at Iris's arrival and commenced a steady stream of chatter regarding his own observations of the encampment while they set up their equipment and portable lab. All he required from Iris was a noise of agreement every now and again.

While most of the analysis of the samples and measurements they took would happen back in the real lab, some things were best handled in the field. And she was lucky enough to work for a firm that could afford the latest in portable geological lab equipment.

She reminded herself of that pertinent fact as her fight-or-flight instincts prompted her toward booking the next plane seat back to the States.

"So, what's the deal between you and the sheikh?" Russell asked when he'd exhausted the topic of the city of tents.

"Sheikh Hakim?" she asked, trying for ignorance.

"Get a grip, Iris. It doesn't take a scientist to interpret the facts. You and Sheikh Asad have some kind of history."

"We went to the same university."

"Right. My freshman year, a CEO of one of the newer dot.coms attended my school. We even met, but that doesn't mean we're friends."

"Asad and I *were* friends." At one time, she'd considered him her very best friend.

And then he'd betrayed her love and her belief in their closeness.

"A whole lot more than that, I'm guessing, or the guy wouldn't have such an effect on you."

"It doesn't matter. The past is exactly that and we're here to—"

"Work. Yeah, yeah, I know." Russell fiddled with a microscope. "You can't blame me for my curiosity. Everyone at CC&B thinks you're more interested in rocks than people, especially men."

He gave her a probing look.

She tried to ignore the pang in her heart that his words gave her. It was true that she hadn't gone out of her way to make friends, and well…rocks couldn't hurt you. But that didn't mean she wasn't interested in people at all.

"I date."

"Really?" he asked with clear disbelief.

Bringing up the one dinner she'd shared with a fellow rock hound in the past year probably wasn't going to count, particularly since all they'd talked about was, well…rocks. "It doesn't matter."

"It does when you're acting like a *woman,* not a scientist."

"That's ridiculous. I'm always a scientist first."

"Sure, until we got here. You offered to let Sheikh Hakim bring in a *male* geologist if it would make him more comfortable." Russell's tone gave that fact the inexplicability it deserved. "This Sheikh Asad had you on the run and he'd only spoken a few words to you."

"I'm not on the run."

"Could have fooled me."

"You're being annoying."

"I'm good at that. You don't usually mind." Russell

stopped looking at his microscope and gave his attention solely to her. "I'm being a nosy friend. So, spill."

It went against the deep sense of privacy she'd always lived with, but then that privacy had left her lonely. Perhaps it was time to make more friends, true friends…not just work acquaintances.

She'd clicked with Russell on both a working and friendship level when he'd first begun his summer internship with CC&B three months ago. She'd been pleased when the college student had been assigned the role of her assistant on this survey.

"Asad and I were together for a few months in my sophomore year," she admitted.

"*Together* together?"

"Yes."

"Wow."

"You didn't suspect?"

"Hell, no. You're not exactly the kind of woman who ends up in a sheikh's bed." The other redhead had the grace to blush at that observation. "I don't mean you're a troll or anything."

"He wasn't a sheikh then."

"I bet he was the same in every other way, though."

"No. He used to smile a lot more."

"Oh-ho."

"Now what?"

"Nothing."

"Stop being cryptic. What is *oh-ho?*"

"You're sad he's not as happy as he used to be. I can tell."

"Don't be an idiot. I didn't say he wasn't happy." But that's what she'd meant and hadn't realized it until Russell brought it up.

"But he's not, is he?"

"His wife died two years ago." And the pampered princess Badra had been nothing like what he'd expected her to be. "He's probably still mourning her."

"Not the way he looks at you, he's not."

She didn't ask what way that was because she already knew and wasn't up to false protestations.

Russell told her anyway. "Like he wants to devour you. If a woman looked at me like that, I'd have a heck of a time staying out of her bed."

"Right." That at least, deserved some proper skepticism. From what she'd seen over the summer, Russell didn't have any more of a social life than she did. "You're as wrapped up in your work as I am."

"But I'd take time away from my precious rocks for something that intense."

"That's why you go clubbing every Saturday night, because you're looking."

"I never go clubbing…oh, you were making a point. I still say if I walked into it like you have here, I'd go for it."

"You wouldn't. You're every bit as gun-shy as I am. You're just being an idiot," she said fondly.

Russell should know just how damaging such a course of action would be to her. He'd had his own broken heart, as he'd confided to her over a bottle of potent wine on their first assignment in the field together.

"You've said that before. Good thing I've got such a high IQ, my confidence in my own intelligence is bulletproof."

She snorted. "IQ measures your ability to learn, not your common sense."

"You saying I lack common sense?"

"If the fossilized fragment fits…"

"Aren't you the clever one?"

"How far from here to our first sampling site?" she asked.

"According to my satellite GPS, about an hour in a Jeep, provided we can travel pretty directly."

She nodded.

"We should ask Sheikh Asad. After all, he is our guide while we're in country."

"He's a sheikh. I'm sure he's got someone else we can go to."

"And you call me an idiot."

"What does that mean?"

"The sheikh's not leaving our guiding up to anyone else and you know it. He wants to handle you…um, I mean this little geological expedition personally."

CHAPTER SIX

IRIS rolled her eyes, but didn't reply to Russell's obvious innuendo.

At any rate, she couldn't exactly deny it. Her field assistant was right. Not only had Asad insisted on being their go-to guy, she was pretty sure he'd want to accompany them on their first foray out of the encampment. She could only hope he would limit himself to the one time.

Her instincts told her to hope all she wanted, but the man was going to become her shadow, big-time busy sheikh or not.

Asad proved her first supposition right later that evening when they were all sharing dinner in his tent.

For the sake of her own sanity, she tried to talk him out of it. "That's not necessary. I've been doing this for almost four years, Asad. I know what I'm doing and Russell can read his pocket transit with the best of them."

"Nawar is looking forward to an excursion. Would you deny her?"

The little girl in question was looking up at Iris with pleading brown eyes.

Oh, not fair. Iris shook her head. "Of course not."

"But can this wait until the day after tomorrow?

Grandmother has planned a welcome feast for your arrival."

"What? Why?"

"You are our guest," Genevieve said, as if that explained everything. "It would be bad manners not to do so."

"But surely Russell and I can start our work tomorrow and return in time for dinner?" she asked, feeling desperate.

She had to get away from Asad's home and remind herself why she was in Kadar.

"It will be much more than a simple meal," Asad said.

Genevieve smiled in a way that was catching. "I thought perhaps you would enjoy witnessing the preparations and this aspect of our way of life."

It would be churlish to refuse, but how Iris wished she could do so. "I would love to. Thank you for the offer."

"I could go on my own and start the measurements," Russell offered.

Surprisingly, it was Asad who shook his head before Iris had a chance to veto the idea. "While traditionally, men do little to prepare the food, we will have our own things to attend to for the feast. You must not miss the opportunity to experience this part of our world."

"Thank you, Sheikh Asad." Russell smiled, his youthful eyes glowing with excitement at the thought. The traitor.

Asad inclined his head.

"Grandmother has said we will have *mansaf.* It's my favorite, but we don't have it very often," Nawar piped up.

"Is it?" Iris asked with a smile for the tiny girl so

unlike her father in looks, but so similar in every other
way. "If I remember correctly, that used to be your father's favorite, too."

She'd even tried to make it for him once, looking up
a recipe online for the traditional stewed lamb and yo-
gurt sauce served over rice. An indifferent cook, Iris
had been disappointed but not surprised when the dish
had turned out only so-so, even to her palate. Asad had
thanked her for the effort, but informed her that traditional Bedouin food had to be prepared in the traditional way—over a campfire—to carry the full flavor.

It was a criticism and excuse for the dinner's medi-
ocrity all-in-one and she hadn't been exactly sure how
to take it. Any hurt feelings she might have had were
dispelled by the passionate lovemaking that followed
dinner, however. He'd made it clear that no matter the
outcome, her efforts had been very much appreciated.

She didn't repeat the mistake of attempting to cook
food from his homeland for him again.

"It still is," Nawar said with a giggle. "Grandmother
says we are just alike."

"I'm sure your grandmother is right." Iris ruffled
Nawar's hair.

"Tomorrow I will show you the baths in the caves,"
Genevieve said. "I'm sure my grandson showed proper
decorum and skipped that part of his tour with you."

Iris didn't know about proper decorum, but the older
woman was right. "Asad didn't mention any baths."

She had to admit to a feeling of relief at the thought
that the next few weeks would not be spent without a
proper soak.

"There are natural hot springs in the caves to the
south of the encampment," Asad said now.

"The women use the upper caves and the men the

lower ones. I suppose they think they can handle the hotter water better," Genevieve said with a loving smile for her husband of several decades. "Hanif discovered them when he was a boy and gifted the caves to the tribe upon our wedding."

It was a romantic story and Iris found herself smiling, as well.

"It just goes to show that for the thousands of years our people have wandered these lands, they remain a mystery to us," Hanif said. He turned to Russell. "Mr. Green, you will join me for coffee in the morning with the other men, yes?"

"Russell, please," her field assistant said with a grin. "And I would be honored. I've been eager to try the real thing ever since I learned we were coming to Kadar."

"Ah, so you understand that what comes out of an automatic drip maker is nothing like it?" Asad asked sardonically with a look at Iris that said he wasn't talking only of coffee.

"I'm willing to be convinced of it," Russell said unsurprisingly. The man was a caffeine addict with a particular fondness for coffee.

If Asad had researched Russell, he couldn't have made a better ploy to get him otherwise occupied in the mornings.

Somehow, regardless of her best efforts, Asad managed to accompany Iris on her trek to her room when it came time to find her bed later that evening.

Which said something about his efforts versus hers, she supposed. Or, perhaps it was the level of determination she should be looking at. The possibility that Asad's might be stronger than hers in this regard was disturbing on more than one level.

She liked the idea that she might not be wholly dedicated to minimizing their contact no better than the thought that he was far more determined to spend time with her than he should be.

"So, what do you think of my city of tents?" he asked just as she reached her doorway and thought to slip inside without incident.

Her hand on the edge of the curtain that covered the entrance to her apartment, Iris stopped. "It's amazing."

"You do not find the remoteness too disconcerting?" he asked with a certain level of disbelief.

A wry smile curved her lips and she met his dark brown gaze squarely. "Asad, last month I spent two weeks in the middle of the East Texas desert doing an updated geological assessment for an oil company. The truth is, your nomadic home is more sophisticated and busy than ninety percent of my assignments."

"Do you enjoy being away from home for such long periods?"

Prepared to give the answer she always offered when asked that question, she was surprised when honesty spilled forth instead. "At least when I'm on assignment, there's a reason for me spending so much time alone."

"Your work."

"Yes."

"It's very important to you."

"It's all I have." She looked around them, noticing his grandparents had already made it into their chamber down the long corridor that ran the width of the tent.

Nawar and Fadwa had gone to bed hours earlier. But still, the sense of family permeated the impressive dwelling.

"We're not all like you, with relations who miss us when we're gone," she added in an even tone.

"Your parents are still living."

"The last time I saw them was Christmas two years ago. We took a winter cruise together." She'd bought it for them as a gift with hopes of building something more of their relationship now that she was an adult.

It hadn't worked. They'd been no more interested in getting to know the grown-up Iris than they had the child. And as much as it hurt to admit, looking at them through adult eyes, she realized her parents were not people she would particularly care to know well, either.

She'd finally given up hope of having anything resembling a real family and hadn't bothered them with so much as an email since. Though now she realized that she'd begun to give up that particular dream when Asad had left.

She simply hadn't been aware of it until her parents' continued indifference pounded the final nail into the coffin that had been her hope.

"Two years ago? But that is criminal. Why would you neglect your parents so shamefully?"

His absolute inability to understand charmed her when she thought probably she should have been offended. But to discover the worldly sheikh so naive in even one area was rather captivating.

"When was the last time you saw your parents?" she asked curiously.

"Last month." He cocked his head to the side, studying her like a specimen under glass. "I travel to Geneva three times a year."

So the decision to allow his grandparents to raise Asad, and groom him to take over as sheikh, had not destroyed their relationship completely. He might resent it somewhat, but he still cared for his parents and she was certain they cared for him, as well.

"Your family is happy to see you when you do, I imagine."

"But naturally."

She nodded. Lucky him. Even after the barbaric bargain, he had parents and siblings who loved him and wanted to see him. And probably a lot more often than the three times a year he went to see them. "For your family, yes. We aren't all so lucky, Asad."

His expression turned thoughtful. "In the ten months of our liaison, you never mentioned a visit from or to your parents. I assumed it was because you saw no reason to introduce me to your family."

It was a reasonable hypothesis, considering the fact Asad himself had not been thinking in terms of a future together. He'd no doubt assumed that while he'd returned home on winter and spring break to see his family, she'd been doing the same. Instead, she'd spent those weeks by herself on campus missing him more than she ever had her parents.

He'd never made any move toward introducing her to anyone in *his* family and because of her past, she hadn't found that odd. Only later had she realized that a man did not introduce his relatives to a casual lover. Particularly not a man slated to one day become sheikh.

Silly her. Iris had thought he was waiting for the right time when the truth was, there was never going to be any such thing for them.

"Once again, I guess we were both guilty of making assumptions." She shook her head, tired and in no mood to prevaricate. "I don't have a family, Asad. I had an egg and sperm donor who were kind enough to financially support me until I graduated from university."

He jerked back as if she'd slapped him. "That is a

very cynical thing to say about the people responsible for giving you life."

"I don't expect you to understand. Your parents allowed your grandparents to raise you in the ways of the Bedouin and while I'm sure you felt abandoned by them, no matter how much you might deny it, the truth is, they never gave you up. Not really. My parents kept legal rights to me, but for all intents and purposes, I was their unwanted ward, not their daughter."

"And you called my grandparents' deal with my parents barbaric," he said in a tone laced with a heavy dose of shocked disapproval.

She just shook her head. He was right. She was in no position to judge and certainly Asad had far more of a family than she did. Though she noticed he didn't deny feeling abandoned by his parents.

He frowned, looking like he wanted to say something more.

She put her hand up in a silent bid for him to leave it. "Like I said, I don't expect you to get it. Why should you? I never did, and they were supposed to be my family. I'm tired and I want to go to bed. All right?"

Though why she was asking him, instead of just going into her room, she didn't really know.

"I don't suppose I could persuade you to share mine," he said in the same teasing tone he used to employ to lighten things when they got too serious when they'd been together.

She'd avoided telling him the truth about her parents because it shamed her to admit she was unloved, but she remembered now the other reason that she'd kept the truth buried. Asad had been so very good at keeping her smiling and happy, she'd been loath to bring the pain of her left-behind childhood into the present.

And, back then, there had still been that tendril of hope that one day her parents were going to realize Iris was someone they could enjoy having in their lives.

She gave him a smile now, not nearly as forced as it should have been. "You're an idiot."

She'd said the same words, or something like them, to Russell earlier, and knew it was because, even after everything, part of her still considered Asad to be a friend.

Perhaps, for a woman like her—who trusted with such difficulty—once trust was given, it could never be withdrawn entirely. The ramifications of that possibility were not good for her heart, not at all.

Unaware of her inner turmoil, Asad gave her a lazy smile she hadn't seen in a very long time. "No, an idiot would let the opportunity slip by."

For a terrible uncertain moment, Iris was tempted to take him up on the offer. She'd never felt like she belonged anywhere like she did in his bed. It had all been a fantasy, but it had *felt* real. In his arms, she'd felt like she had a family.

And it had almost killed her to lose him.

She wasn't setting herself up for that again. She couldn't.

She didn't bother to reply, but simply slipped into her room. Tying the cords that would keep the curtain snugly over her doorway while she slept, she ignored the tears tracking down her cheeks.

The next day, as much as she tried to hold herself aloof, Iris found herself falling under the spell of the four-year-old daughter as easily as she had the father six years before. Nawar had spent the entire day, except her nap, acting as Iris's shadow.

It had been a busy day, filled with preparations for the feast and chatter with Asad's female relatives.

Iris had enjoyed herself so much that she'd felt guilty for not working, despite the fact a phone call from Sheikh Hakim had made it clear that he did not expect Iris to begin her geological assessment until after she'd been officially welcomed into the city of tents.

Now that the food and party preparations were over, Genevieve had told Iris it was time for their personal preparations. Iris had intended to wear the single dress she'd brought with her for what she'd believed was to be a remote field assignment, but Genevieve would not hear of it.

She and Nawar had made a big production out of choosing a galabia from Genevieve's wardrobe for Iris to wear to the feast. And the small girl had now appointed herself as Iris's instructor in the ways of bathing in the communal baths of the Sha'b Al'najid.

They were now soaking in the largest of the pools fed by an underground hot springs in the women's section of the caves, after a cursory wash with fragrant soap and water left to cool in large bowls near the pools.

"You must rest. No splashing or swimming," the small girl said with a very serious mien. "After a long time, we wash again with the sand from the bottom of the pool."

Iris wondered what a long time meant to a small child and smiled. "I bet that makes your skin very soft."

Nawar gave her a solemn nod. "Grandmother says so."

"And our hair?" She'd found it odd that they didn't shampoo before coming into the communal pool of mineral waters.

"We're supposed to wash it first," Nawar admitted with a frown.

Oho, the little one didn't like washing her hair. "Don't you want your hair soft like your skin and shiny like silk?"

"The soap gets in my eyes." Nawar gave a childish pout. "It stings."

"I think I can help you wash your hair without getting soap in your eyes."

"Fadwa tries, but she says I move too much," Nawar replied doubtfully.

"You seem very good at staying still now."

"Thank you." Nawar gave Iris a guilty look. "I don't like to wash my hair."

"So, perhaps you move more when Fadwa is trying to get it clean than you should, hmmm?"

"Maybe."

Iris nodded. "Well, you will simply have to do better for me, because if I get soap in your eyes it will make me very sad."

"I don't want you to be sad."

"Thank you."

Iris successfully washed the child's long dark hair without getting soap or water in her eyes after their soak and then sand scrubbing. Nawar was ecstatic and begged Iris to promise to wash her hair from now on.

"As long as I am here, I will. All right?" More than that, Iris could not promise.

They dressed for the party in the bathing caves after drying and brushing their hair. Genevieve had insisted on lending Iris a sheer silk scarf to be worn over her head and around her shoulders in the traditional manner. It matched exactly the heavily embroidered peacock-blue galabia she'd given Iris to wear earlier.

Walking back to the sheikh's tent, Iris felt like an Arabian princess.

"I have not seen that galabia in a long time," Asad's grandfather said when Iris and Nawar entered the dwelling. "It was always one of my favorites."

"Oh…I shouldn't have worn it, but Genevieve insisted," Iris said, feeling awkward.

"Nonsense." The old sheikh gave her a rakish smile and Iris could see what had attracted Genevieve all those years ago. "Naturally my wife chose it for you to wear. It is the perfect color to bring out the cream of your skin and that red shine in your hair so uncommon among our people. The other guests will be in awe of the beauty of the women of my house."

Iris blushed at the praise.

"I agree, Grandfather. The peacock galabia is lovely on Iris." The words were complimentary, but Asad gave his grandmother what couldn't be mistaken for anything but an admonishing look.

The older woman returned his gaze, her own serene. "Nawar chose it."

Asad's brow rose. "It is the traditional dress of the women of my house."

It had seemed rather a coincidence that the brightly colored trim around the skirt of Nawar's little party dress was styled after peacock feathers. And Genevieve's peach silk galabia had peacocks amidst the intricate gold needlework covering the garment. Even Fadwa's dress had tiny peacock feathers embroidered along the hem.

Iris's borrowed galabia was not only the shade of blue in a peacock feather, but had the birds embroidered on either side of the collar with sequins stitched into the tail feathers. More stitching ran around the collar, down the center of the garment and around the hem.

It was one of the most beautiful things Iris had ever worn.

Nevertheless, she should probably go change. "I'm not a member of your house. I shouldn't be wearing this."

"You are our guest." Which seemed to be Asad's answer to everything. "It is fine."

"But—"

"It is your favorite color." He reached out and tweaked his daughter's hair. "Nawar is partial to that shade of blue, as well. It is no wonder she chose this dress."

"I like purple best, though," Nawar said with a smile for her father.

"I know you do, little jewel." He met Iris's gaze then, his own somewhat rueful but unmovable. "It would be an insult to my grandmother to refuse to wear the gala-bia she offered you."

Knowing she wasn't about to win that particular argument, Iris gave in gracefully and smiled at Genevieve. "Peacocks are my favorite bird. It isn't just the color. Thank you for letting me wear this beautiful garment."

"No thanks are necessary. You must keep it if you like it," Genevieve said firmly. "I would have given it to Badra long ago, but she preferred Western dress."

"Oh, no. I couldn't take it." Particularly not a dress that was to have been passed down from Genevieve to the woman who had wed her grandson.

"But you must. You will offend my wife if you do not," the old sheikh said with that all-too-familiar arrogance.

Like grandfather, like grandson. Iris found herself amused instead of annoyed by the overt manipulations. Particularly when she saw the look Asad gave the old sheikh.

For whatever reason, it appeared he felt like he was being maneuvered just as neatly as she was. That couldn't help but make it easier for her to accept his grandmother's generosity.

Iris found herself grinning and winked at the old man. "We can't have that, can we? I would be honored to accept such a lovely gift," she said to Genevieve.

"Your old college friend is impertinent, Asad. Did you see her wink at this old man?" Hanif asked.

"I saw," Asad said with one of his infrequent smiles. "Grandmother will have to keep her eyes open at to-night's feast."

"Oh, you." Genevieve slapped her grandson's arm lightly. "Don't encourage him. He'll be flirting with the tourists again."

"The tourists love me. A desert sheikh of the old ways." Hanif pointed at himself importantly.

"I'm sure they do," Iris said with a smile, letting her gaze slide to Asad.

She imagined the tourists loved him as well, especially the women. Did he flirt with them like his grandfather? If Asad did, it wouldn't be innocent fun like with the old man—of that Iris was certain.

Realizing she really didn't want to think about Asad flirting with and conducting liaisons with the tourists, or anyone else for that matter, Iris forced all thoughts of the like from her mind.

CHAPTER SEVEN

THE feast was far more than a simple dinner, just as Asad had said it would be.

Platter after platter of food came in from the outdoor kitchens—far more than the ones Iris had helped Genevieve and the cook prepare the other night. The other women in the courtyard had all been cooking as well, but Iris hadn't known it had been for the feast.

They ate in the public receiving area of Asad's tent, the large room filled with his family and guests who Iris learned were all related to him, if distantly.

Russell, who had been seated at a different table from the immediate family, didn't seem in the least offended, but appeared to be enjoying himself every bit as much as Iris was.

After everyone had eaten, the men played their instruments and sang traditional songs, some stories of love and romance, other songs Nawar told Iris were for the camels.

"It helps them to be strong and carry heavy burdens," the small girl explained very seriously.

Iris nodded her understanding, though she found the idea fanciful.

Even Asad joined in the singing, his deep masculine voice making the song of love lost he'd chosen to share unexpectedly poignant. Then he sang a song in a dialect Iris did not understand, but the cadence of the song and tone of his voice made her thighs quiver with unwanted longing.

Her discomfort only increased when several of the guests gave her assessing glances. She tried looking everywhere but at Asad. Only his voice inexorably drew her gaze back to him.

He met her eyes, singing the last stanza in a low, melodic tone that brought moisture to her eyes, which she did her best to blink away.

"You enjoyed my humble efforts?" he asked Iris as he allowed Nawar to climb into his lap and rest against his chest.

The small girl had been allowed to stay up past her bedtime and looked ready to fall asleep right where she was.

Iris caught herself staring at the charming domestic picture they made as she answered, "Just as I'm sure everyone does who hears you. You're a man of many talents."

Iris's desire to be part of that scene was so strong, her chest ached with it. Though she knew there was no hope of that ever happening. She wasn't Asad's future.

No doubt there was another perfect princess in store for him, hopefully one with a stronger character than the deceased Badra.

"I am glad to hear you say so."

"I'm sure you hear it often enough."

"Perhaps."

She huffed out a small laugh at his arrogance. "You don't lack confidence, that's for sure."

"And do you think there is a reason why I should?"

"No, Asad, you are everything a desert sheikh should be."

"My daddy is the bestest sheikh ever," Nawar said, her tiredness showing in the childish pattern of speech so rarely exhibited by the young girl.

"Even better than Sheikh Hakim?" Iris teased. "After all, he is king over all of Kadar."

"Daddy is sheikh to the Sha'b Al'najid," Nawar said around a yawn. "That's bestest."

"I suppose it is, sweetheart."

The little girl's eyelids drooped.

"So, why is the peacock the symbol for your house when your tribe is called the people of the lion?" Iris asked Asad.

Even he had been named for the large predatory animal.

"The peacock is a symbol for the *women* of my house."

"But it's on the panel that leads to the…" And then Iris understood. "It covers the doorway that leads to what is traditionally considered the women's chamber."

"Yes."

"So, how did a bird become the symbol for the women of your house?"

"Many generations ago, one of the first sheikhs of our line, gave a peacock and peahen pair to his bride as a wedding gift. They were very exotic birds, something none of the Bedouin of their tribe had ever seen though as nomadic people they saw more wonders than the settled dwellers of our part of the world."

"Where did he get the birds?"

"I do not know, but his wife was so taken with them that she embroidered their likeness on all of her clothing."

Nawar made a soft little snoring sound and Iris couldn't help smiling. "And it became tradition to do so in the following generations."

"It did, though not all adhere to this tradition any longer."

"Why do you?"

"I did not, for a while, but my grandmother finds the birds beautiful, even the less-flamboyant peahen."

"Badra was not as impressed with the tradition," Iris guessed.

Asad's featured turned stern. "She was a princess of a neighboring country, but she preferred Western ways to anything the desert had to offer."

"Even you."

"Even me." Asad's clenched his jaw and Iris felt badly for reminding him that his marriage had not turned out anything like he'd anticipated when he'd dumped her to marry the virginal princess.

"I'm sorry. I shouldn't have said that."

"It is the truth."

"I'm still sorry."

"Come with me to put her to bed," he invited, indicating his sleeping daughter.

Iris nodded before her brain could even finish processing the request. She shouldn't. She knew she shouldn't. Keeping her distance from him was the only hope she had of keeping her heart intact this time around.

But keeping her distance from his daughter simply wasn't an option. After the years of rejection at her parents' hands, Iris did not have it in her to disappoint the child.

Besides, she liked Nawar.

Iris helped Asad undress Nawar and put a nightgown

on the sleeping child like she'd done it a hundred times before. It should feel awkward, but it didn't. Maybe the old saying was true, some things were just like riding a bicycle. You never really forgot how to do them, no matter how young you were when you learned.

While Iris had no experience with children as an adult, in boarding school she had often taken care of the younger ones.

She tucked the little girl into her bed, soothing her back to sleep with a soft lullaby when Nawar started to wake after her father laid her down.

"You're good with her," Asad said as they left the room moments later.

"Thank you. I've had some experience."

"I wasn't aware you had small children in your life." He talked like he knew a lot more about her life than he possibly could.

"I don't."

"But you've had experience?" he prompted.

"I learned how to tuck little girls in when I was a child myself."

"Explain," he pushed.

"My parents sent me to boarding school when I was six. I was terrified at night without our housekeeper there to tuck me in and tell me a story."

"I know this is a common practice, sending away one's children, but not one I could ever approve of for my own."

She didn't imagine a man who considered family as important as Asad did would. That knowledge cemented her certainty that his parents' defection to Geneva had hurt him badly, though he might never acknowledge it.

"It's actually not as frequent a practice in America as

it is in England, particularly not for children as young as I was, but there are some schools who will board their students from the age of six."

"And your parents saw fit to send you to one of these?"

"Yes."

"But how does that explain your experience with small children?"

"When I had been there a year, another six-year-old girl came to board, as well. Though I was second youngest of all the boarders, I was seven then and used to the life. The rest of the children in our grades were day schoolers."

"Day schoolers?"

"They came for the day, not to live."

"I see." He stopped her before they returned to the feast. "But you were a night schooler? No that would not be right."

She smiled at his attempt to get the word right. "I was a resident, or a boarder."

"Oh, yes, of course. And this little girl…"

"They put her in my room because we were so close in age. I could hear her crying in her bed that first night. She missed her parents terribly."

"So, you comforted her?"

"I had a little flashlight. I used it to read her a book. Then I sang to her until she fell asleep." Iris had returned to her own bed after that, more comforted than she had been at bedtime since going to the school.

"It became a routine."

"Yes. She was only there for a semester. Her parents had been in an accident and couldn't care for her, but as soon as they could, they came and got her."

Iris had been without a roommate until the next

year, when they'd put the two newest and youngest residents in a room with her again, since she'd been so good with her other roommate. "The girls' dormitory mother made sure that the youngest residents were always put in my room."

"Even when you were older? That must have put a cramp in your style."

Iris laughed. "Not so you would notice. I was a very shy girl, but I knew how to comfort the little ones and help them transition to boarding school life."

"They were lucky to have you."

"It was mutual. I would have been very lonely otherwise."

"Didn't you have friends?"

"Of course."

"But not close ones," he guessed far too perceptively.

"I made the mistake of growing close to a couple of girls in the beginning, but then they left." And she'd learned not to let people get too close.

They always left. But then Asad had come along and she'd opened her heart again…only, he'd left too.

"And now?"

"Now?"

"Do you have friends now?" he asked in a strangely tense voice.

"Russell."

"*Russell?* Your assistant?"

"You say his name like it's a dirty word. He's a really great guy." Iris liked the geological assistant who told corny jokes only another geologist would get.

"Are you attracted to this really great guy?" Asad asked with dangerous quiet. "He is a great deal younger than you."

A junior at his university, Russell was about as much

SAVE UP TO 25%

Subscribe to Modern today and get 4 books a month
delivered to your door for 3, 6 or 12 months and gain
up to 25% OFF! That's a fantastic saving of over £40!

MONTHS	FULL PRICE	YOUR PRICE	SAVING
3	£41.88	£35.61	15%
6	£83.76	£67.02	20%
12	£167.52	£125.64	25%

As a welcome gift we will also
send you a FREE L'Occitane
gift set worth £10

**PLUS, by becoming a member you
will also receive these additional benefits:**

🌹 FREE Home Delivery

🌹 Receive new titles TWO MONTHS AHEAD of the shops

🌹 Exclusive Special Offers & Monthly Newsletter

🌹 Special Rewards Programme

No Obligation - You can cancel your subscription at any time by writing
to us at Mills & Boon Book Club, PO Box 676, Richmond. TW9 1WU.

To subscribe, visit
millsandboon.co.uk/subscriptions

younger than Iris as she had been than Asad when they
were together. "He's twenty. Anyway, what difference
does it make to you?"

"Answer me. Are you two in a relationship?" he said,
the last word laced with disgust.

She rolled her eyes. "If I didn't know better, I'd think
you were jealous."

"Who says I am not?"

She laughed, the sound cynical. "Oh, come on,
Asad. Like you are going to be jealous of a geeky science boy."

"Are you attracted to geeky?"

She could have been, she realized. Not Russell, necessarily. He was very much like a younger brother, but
maybe to someone else like that. If there hadn't been
Asad to spoil her for others. "You asked me if I had
friends, Asad. That's what he is. My friend."

And a pretty new one at that.

"Good."

"I'm glad you think so."

"But you *don't* have a lot of friends back home."

"No."

"Yet you are a very good friend to have."

She made a sound of disbelief. If he'd really believed
that, he wouldn't have given her up so easily. Would he?

"You were my friend once. It was only later that I
realized what I lost when that friendship had to end."

"There was no *had to,* Asad. You were done with me
and you dumped me. Stop trying to rewrite history."

"I am doing no such thing. Do you really think we
could have remained friends when I married Badra?"

He had a point. And Iris probably shouldn't care that
he'd missed her friendship, and yet coming to believe
it dulled some of the old pain of losing him.

"I would like to be friends again," he said when she made no reply.

She didn't believe him. "You want me back in your bed. That's not friendship."

"For us it can be."

"Really? And when I return to the States, what then?"

"I do not intend to eject you from my life again," he said in a tone that made the words a vow.

It disconcerted her, and frightened her, as well. Because those words were not merely a promise…they were a threat, too. "I don't think I'm any more prepared to be your friend after leaving here than I was before."

What she meant, but didn't say, and hoped he clued into, was that for Iris it had been more than casual sex and friendship. And unfortunately, probably always would be.

"Give it a try. Let us see where it goes."

It wouldn't go to the altar; at least this time she knew that. Knowledge of the truth had to make some kind of difference in the outcome, didn't it?

"You want me in your bed."

"I do." At least he admitted it.

"And you want to be my friend." For now, anyway.

"Yes."

"What will that make us?" she asked uncertainly.

"Whatever we want it to."

This time she heard what he said, not what she wanted to hear. He wasn't making any promises.

She wanted to be his world like he'd been hers, but that was never going to happen. What did she say to this offer, though? She'd missed Asad so much because she'd let him into a place in her heart she'd kept protected from her very earliest childhood.

Now he was offering more than a tumble in the sack.

He was offering a renewal of their friendship that supposedly would last into the future.

She wasn't sure she wanted that to happen, but she was equally unsure if she wanted to hold herself back from him while she was in Kadar. Iris had spent six years avoiding intimacy, taking no other lovers and dreaming of Asad more nights than she cared to count.

Could having what he called a liaison with him help her to let go of him forever? Just being away from him hadn't done the trick. Psychobabble said people needed closure to move on. If she ever wanted to break the lonely boundaries of her life, Iris had to move forward. She had to take a chance again.

So, maybe that was exactly what she needed…closure on a relationship that was never meant to be in the first place.

One truth she could not escape: Iris had missed this man every day since he had walked away.

Losing him the first time had nearly destroyed her, but maybe being with him again, knowing it was temporary, would help to heal her now. Maybe letting him in again was the only way to break the boundaries she'd set around her lonely life.

She'd like to believe she could refuse him, but recognized that putting it to the test might see her disappointed. Regardless, she realized she didn't really want to.

Understanding better what had been going through his head six years ago—and realizing how betrayed he'd been by Badra—changed Iris's view of their shared past. At the very least, it made her realize Asad was not invulnerable to hurt.

Why that should matter, she was not sure, but it did. And she wanted him, more than she would have believed possible after everything that had happened. But there it was.

She had a choice, one that only she could make. If she got back into Asad's bed, it would be with her eyes open to both the reality of the past and what the future would hold.

Could she live with that? She thought maybe she really could. She was almost positive she *couldn't* live with the other…the not having him and the richness he brought to her life for whatever time available to them.

When the silence stretched between them as her thoughts whirled inside her head, Asad slipped his hand beneath the scarf covering her head and cupped her nape. "It is not in me to lose you again."

Asad saw the flash of disbelief in Iris's blue gaze before she pushed the peacock curtain aside to return to the feast.

He wanted to draw her back, demand she acknowledge the truth of his claim, but now was not the time. She was skittish, and perhaps he understood that better now. But he would woo her and convince her that the past's mistakes could be left there.

He had brought her to Kadar for the reason he'd given her, to help her career, but also because he'd never forgotten her. Not her friendship and not her passionate fire in the bedroom.

He wanted to be warmed by that fire again.

Where that might lead, he did not know, but one certainty existed. He was no longer looking for a perfect princess to share his life.

Iris's reflections on her childhood horrified him. If the two lived among the Sha'b Al'najid, they would have lost not just their daughter, but also their place in the tribe for such unnatural behavior. That parents could be so dismissive of a child was bad enough, but that the child should be his sensitive former lover infuriated him.

One of the first things he had noticed about Iris was the vulnerability she hid behind her shy demeanor. The sensitive child she would have been must have been tormented endlessly by her parents' indifference.

He could not fathom it.

Iris had been right. Asad had not been pleased at his own father's rejection of their heritage and he had determined at a young age never to make a choice that required leaving a child behind, as his parents had him. Yet Asad had never felt ignored by his parents, or that he did not matter to them.

They had made the journey back to the Sha'b Al'najid much more frequently than was convenient for them in order to spend time with their oldest son. And while they had agreed Asad would be raised to be sheikh of his people one day, his father had demanded Asad be allowed to come to Geneva at least one weekend per month throughout his childhood.

Though Asad was not supposed to know it, his mother cried when he left—each and every time.

Still, Asad had fought against more frequent visits, even at the earliest age. He was sure now that his parents had been hurt by that, but then the choice to leave the Sha'b Al'najid—and him, their son—had been theirs.

Regardless, they had been so different from the soulless couple who had given life to his beautiful geologist.

His parents' choice had cost them. Of that he was certain, despite the fact he was equally certain he could never have made that choice himself. The thought of letting Nawar go had been thoroughly untenable from the first time he held her, despite the fact that they shared no actual blood tie.

An inexplicable protectiveness burning in his gut, Asad kept Iris by his side during the rest of the feast, thoroughly enjoying her reaction to his family's way of celebrating.

Badra had always found the ways of the Sha'b Al'najid provincial and never hesitated to say so. The youngest, spoiled daughter of a neighboring country's king, she had rejected Asad's first proposal, saying she would never marry an ignorant goatherd.

Asad, who at eighteen had herded the animals only to learn lessons his grandfather said could not be taught with words, was hugely offended. And equally intrigued by this beautiful, spoiled creature who thought she was too good for him.

Any among the women of his people, or those he had met visiting his parents in Switzerland, would have been more than honored to receive such an offer of marriage. Badra, who was a year his senior, had unaccountably turned him down.

She couldn't have conceived a move more suited to garnering his interest and determination to woo her successfully.

They'd met during a trade negotiation between Asad's grandfather and Badra's father. As was custom, the negotiations had occurred in the home of the king wanting his grandfather's services in moving goods between his country and those nearby.

Asad had found the city-bred and sophisticated young woman fascinating. Besides, she *was* a princess, and as a future sheikh, he should marry a woman of such standing.

Asad allowed himself a small, bitter smile at his own naïveté and arrogance.

Badra had not been impressed with his pedigree, thereby cementing his interest in her. Then and there, he had determined to win her hand. He would attend university and build his tribe into a people others would envy.

And that the Princess Badra would want to belong to.

So he'd gone to university and graduate school, all the while working to build his family's business interests with the help of his father and grandfather. When Asad returned to his desert family permanently, he was determined to do so with Badra at his side.

The only stumbling block to that outcome had been his growing affection for his lover, Iris Carpenter. But a man of considerable will, Asad had forced himself to cut her out of his life and pursue his original goal. It was what was best for his people.

Badra's father would make a powerful political and business ally, the innocent and protected Badra a beautiful and admired lady of his people.

He shook his head. He'd been a fool.

Asad had not been in the least surprised when she accepted his second proposal. He'd assumed her father had convinced her of the advantageousness of the match. It was on Asad's wedding night that he'd discovered the true reason for Badra's capitulation.

Far from the innocent virgin he'd expected to bed, Badra was well versed in the art of sexual encounters.

She was also pregnant. Which he had realized when she woke the next morning nauseated in a way he had witnessed only among the pregnant women of his tribe.

He'd demanded to know the truth and she'd admitted everything amid floods of tears.

She'd had an affair with a married man who had seduced her from her innocence and now carried the man's child. She said she was terrified of what her father's reaction would be if he found out. Claiming to always have a soft spot for Asad, she said she'd learned her lesson and had eagerly accepted his marriage proposal.

She didn't think she was doing him any true harm, as she'd discovered the babe's sex was female. He would not reject a daughter simply because she had come to be as the result of her mother's ignorance and naïveté, would he?

She played to Asad's view of himself as a modern man who knew how to straddle the old world and the new. And he accepted her explanations and perceptions of him because his pride would not allow him to do otherwise, swallowing her words like a camel at an oasis after five days in the desert.

Though he had not forgotten the contempt she'd held for him at eighteen, he believed she had changed her views. He even accepted the role his own pride had played in the current circumstances. He'd been adamant he would marry this woman and no other. She would not reject him, the lion of his people.

He had put himself forward as her unknowing savior and he could hardly withdraw from the field at this point.

Badra claimed she'd broken it off with the married man when she agreed to become the lady of the Sha'b Al'najid, but he'd had his doubts—unspoken and unacknowledged. However, he'd made his vows just as she had. With that truth firmly in the forefront of his mind, Asad had directed his considerable will toward making his marriage with Badra work.

His doubts had come to fruition a month after Nawar's birth when Asad's head of security in the newly created command center had informed him of communications between Badra and her former lover.

But the knowledge of her continued perfidy had come too late. Asad loved his daughter and would not lose her to her mother's selfishness.

He had not realized until much later, in a discussion with his sister during her first pregnancy, that Badra could not possibly have known the babe in her womb was a girl on their wedding night. Not unless she'd had an amniocentesis, which she had not. Badra had been a consummate liar.

And for the sake of *that woman* and his own pride, Asad had let go of his friendship with the one woman whose loyalty and integrity had never once come into question.

Unlike Badra with her deceits and machinations, Iris would always put others first. It was in her nature to do so. Knowing more about her past, he found that trait even more worthy of admiration.

CHAPTER EIGHT

For the second night in a row, Iris found herself walking with Asad toward her room at bedtime. It was much later this night though, the last of Asad's guests having just left.

"There is one chamber you have yet to see in my home," he said as they reached her door.

She'd spent the last hours of the party wrestling with what to do about Asad and had come to a decision.

One thing was certain—he wasn't giving up. She knew how determined he could be and was under no illusions that this time would be any different. He wanted her. He would do his best to get what he wanted.

She could spend the next few weeks doing her level best to avoid him and stifle her own desire for him, but she was not convinced of her own ultimate success.

If she let herself love him again, she was lost. There was another option though, wasn't there?

She'd come to believe that sharing his bed again would help heal her heart. Sometimes the only way to rebirth in life was through the fire. Just like a Phoenix. She would be the one to leave this time and because of that she would not spend the next six years seeing his face every time she looked with interest at another man.

She'd come to the conclusion that the way out of the

isolated existence her life had become was the same way into it. Through Asad. This time she knew he wasn't looking for a future with her and she would not allow herself to look for one either...or fall in love with him again.

That would dictate the difference in the outcome. It had to.

"You're right." Her voice was husky, but not tentative. One thing her feelings about this man had never been was tentative. "I haven't seen your room."

"Would you like to?"

"It will not offend your grandparents?" Iris was not naive enough to believe they would not figure it out, even if she left Asad's bed in the wee hours as she meant to.

This kind of thing always seemed to get out eventually. Physical intimacy had a way of showing itself, even when those involved did their best to hide it. And Asad was too proud and arrogant to even try.

Iris was no good at hiding her emotions, even if she wanted to. She would show the change in her relationship with the sheikh, even if she did her best not to.

He pulled her around to face him, his expression dark and serious. "I am sheikh now. There is no offense in me doing as I see fit in my own home."

She took leave to doubt that culturally it was easy as that, but then this man lived by his own rules, no matter how traditionally Bedouin he could be at times.

"Your arrogance is showing again."

"I am certain of my place."

She nodded, for the moment equally certain of hers. "Show me."

His nostrils flared and his eyes burned her. "It will be my pleasure."

"If I remember right, the pleasure was always very mutual."

"Yes."

He led her into his room and she was surprised to discover that the chamber was the same size as hers, but the bed was much bigger. Covered in pillows and a silk quilt embroidered with a roaring male lion in the center, it was easily twice the width of her bed. Between it and the sparse furniture, there was no extra room as in her chamber.

The sound of rustling clothes had her looking back toward him only to discover he was already disrobing, his *kuffiya* discarded, revealing dark hair that framed his fierce features even better than the head covering had done. He'd also tossed off the ornate robe he'd worn to the feast. Under it he had on the traditional loose trousers and...*an Armani shirt?*

She grinned.

"What?" he asked, arrested in his movements while looking at her.

"You're wearing Armani with your traditional garb."

He shrugged. "I prefer their shirts." He dropped his trousers. "And their shorts."

Her breath caught in her throat at the sight of his muscular legs. Darker than they used to be, and rippling with even more muscle she wanted to touch.

There was a time when she had believed that body belonged to her. She knew now that it did not, but she could still revel in the knowledge that as long as she shared his bed, for all intents and purposes, it might as well be hers.

"Nice," she said, unable to hide the catch in her voice.

His hardness pressed against the black silk of his

Armani boxers, letting her know that his desire for her was real. He unbuttoned the shirt, letting it fall open to reveal the sprinkling of black curls that lightly covered his chest and abdomen.

"You used to shave that," she observed.

He frowned momentarily. "I was trying to be more urbane."

"But why would you want to? You were always so proud of your heritage." It was one of many things about him that had impressed her.

Asad had known who and what he was in a way she had still been trying to achieve for herself. But maybe, he hadn't had it as together as she'd believed. That knowledge cast the past in a different light once again, one that eased old hurts even further.

She'd made the right decision to let him make love to her. This coming together *would* be healing…it already was.

"Another time, we will discuss these things." He moved toward her. "But now is not the time for talking."

She wouldn't argue. It had been six years since she felt the level of excitement coursing through her body now and he hadn't even kissed her yet.

He rectified that with a swift movement, bringing their bodies flush and their mouths together in perfect union. Passion and need exploded inside her with nuclear power.

Everything she'd been suppressing for six years, but especially over the past two days broke through her mental restraints, making her body strain against his even as her lips gave him kiss for kiss, caress for caress.

He broke his mouth from hers, gasping. "It's been so long. Too long."

She had to agree. "Yes."

"For you, as well?" he asked, his brown eyes almost black with the depth of his feeling.

And she could not deny him the truth. "For me, too."

It had definitely been too long since she touched him, as the depth of her excitement showed. They'd had one explosive kiss and she felt like it would take only the slightest touch to her intimate flesh for her to climax.

He'd always known just how to touch her to bring her the ultimate in pleasure, but this was something different. This bliss was coming from deep inside her at the knowledge that, for a little while, they were going to be one again.

But she would not love him. Not this time. Their bodies would join, but not their hearts. She was too smart for that. *Please, God, let her be too smart for that.*

He shrugged his shirt off. "Come with me to my bed. Let us make new memories to supplant the old."

He knew exactly what to say, but that should not surprise her. Other than when he dumped her, Asad had always known exactly what she needed to hear from him.

"New memories," she agreed breathlessly as he gently pulled away the scarf covering her hair.

"I always loved your hair, the red is so rich and unique. It feels like liquid silk." He combed through it with his fingers, his expression intent.

"That's the shampoo and conditioner I use," she said with a smile.

"You think?"

She nodded. She wasn't a vain woman, she didn't think, but Iris had always insisted on using salon quality products on her hair. The way it slipped through Asad's fingers now made her little idiosyncrasy worth it.

"I think it is the magic of the woman, myself."

"You think I'm magic?" she asked softly, tears stinging her eyes that she *would not* let fall.

"I do." He stopped with his hands poised to undress her. "You are sure you want this?"

She was shocked by his question, but maybe she should not have been. No matter how determined Asad was, he was and had always been a man of honor.

She nodded.

"We will erase the ugly memories of the past."

"What memories are you trying to erase?" she couldn't help asking, though she so wanted to move forward with the seduction.

He shrugged, but then surprised her by following it up with words. "You were the last woman I bedded that brought nothing but honesty to our time together."

"You were honest, too." Though for a long time, she'd thought he hadn't been.

"Yes."

"So, this is a reset? For both of us?"

"Yes."

She got that. He'd been hurt badly by Badra's infidelity, Iris was sure. Asad wanted to go back to a time when he could trust the woman in his bed. Iris wanted the same thing. "Then, I'm sure."

He nodded and then removed her galabia with reverent hands, his expression unreadable, but intense and primitive.

Was that possession glowing in his brown gaze? Or desire?

It didn't matter. For a few brief hours, she would let her body be his, just not her heart.

He reached behind her to unclasp her bra. "You still wear such feminine underwear beneath your T-shirts and jeans."

"I wasn't wearing jeans tonight."

"But you brought this with you regardless." He drew the silky champagne lace bra down her arms and dropped it to the carpet under their feet.

She couldn't deny it. She might dress like an asexual scientist most of the time, but underneath, her bras and panties were her one consistent feminine indulgence.

His large hands cupped her breasts, his thumbs brushing over her hardened nipples.

She sucked in a breath.

Approval flared in his dark eyes. "So responsive."

His gaze dipped low and she felt the caress of his eyes on her most sensitive flesh, though it was still hidden behind the stretch lace boy shorts that matched her bra. "This style is new for you. I like it."

"It's been six years since you've seen my underwear."

"I'm keen to see what else you have in store for me."

Which implied this was not a onetime deal. And she'd known that. He'd said as much when admitting he wanted her back in his bed, but this further proof that tonight was not their only and last night together still settled over her in an unexpected delight.

"Take off your panties," he ordered in a guttural tone.

"Why don't you?"

"I can't stop touching you." The admission affected something deep inside her she didn't want reached and she almost pulled away.

But the way he played so intently with her breasts, giving her pleasure and so obviously taking his own from the caresses, made it impossible for her to deny him. Or herself.

Soon, they were both naked and lying together in the big bed, the covers tossed back. His hands mapping her body as if memorizing it, comparing it to memory and marking all the similarities and differences.

She could not remember a time they had made love before when he had been so intent on learning her every dip and crevice. Not even their first time together.

Something about tonight was different for him too, but she wasn't about to speculate what that might be. She'd make the wrong assumptions as she'd done before and her heart couldn't afford such mistakes again.

He leaned up over her, his regard serious. "You are the first woman I have brought to this bed."

But he'd been married. "Badra?"

"Had her own room."

Iris couldn't imagine him having sex with his wife on that tiny bed, so Badra's bed must have gone the way of her other things.

"Do you want me to be flattered?" she asked and then wished she could take back the facetious comment.

It might not be love, but this moment was too profound for sarcasm.

His tender smile said he was not offended. "It is I who am honored to have you here."

So that was what he wanted, for her to feel honored by the distinction. And really? She did. Not that she was going to tell him so. It seemed like too much an admission to make after she'd opened herself to him in a way she'd been determined never to again.

"Kiss me, Asad."

He did, a growl of desire sounding between them, his body moving over hers in that dominating way he'd always had. An aggressive lover, Asad filled her senses with his presence as he caressed her body with the clear intent to seduce and excite. He knew how to draw forth more than she ever intended to give and yet fill her with bliss in the way she responded to him.

She returned his touches, reveling in her ability to once again lay claim to the magnificent man above her.

Their kisses were incendiary, the fire burning inside her in no danger of being extinguished. Tense with need, her body remembered this man's lovemaking and the capacity for pleasure he had taught her that she had.

He brought her to her first climax with his hand, his lips never leaving hers. Once he had swallowed all her cries as his due, he moved down her body, his mouth blazing a trail of heat and want that culminated in a renewed pulsing in the tender flesh between her thighs.

She found completion the second time with his mouth on her, his tongue lashing her clitoris with deft flicks, his hands roving her body and settling on her breasts as he manipulated her nipples to enhance her pleasure until she screamed with it.

She grabbed a pillow to stifle her cries, but he reared up and yanked it from her hand. "I want to hear every sound. I will have all of you."

"But the tent walls…"

"Are far better at muffling sound than you would ever imagine, my sweet little Westerner."

"That was the problem, wasn't it?" she asked, her body still shuddering from the ultimate in pleasure, his resting between her wantonly spread thighs. "I was too Western for your people. Like your mother."

"My grandmother was from the West, as well. She adapted."

"But her son did not."

"No. Why are we talking about my parents right now?" he asked as he thrust his hard and very impressive member against her.

"Because…" She let her voice trail off, unsure what she wanted to say, what she was willing to admit to.

Even though she didn't want to be, she'd been trying to understand how he could let something so good go. What they'd had between them had been incredible, not just something that worked to relieve sexual tension.

"I might have been innocent, but even I knew we were amazing together. The sex was mind-blowing from the very first time." And so had everything else between them been.

The dip of his head acknowledged the truth of her words.

"Why?" she asked, finally able to do so.

"I planned to marry Badra from the time I was eighteen." And he was the type of man that when he had a plan, he stuck to it. Could it really have been that simple?

When she didn't reply, he added, "There was no lack in you. Nothing missing from *us*."

She just hadn't been the Middle Eastern princess he'd wanted. "When you dumped me, I sure felt lacking."

"No." He kissed the join between her neck and shoulder, suckling up a love bite, and sent pleasure zinging through her. "You were the perfect lover."

But not the perfect candidate for wife, even if Badra hadn't been in the wings waiting. That much Iris understood.

Unwilling to dwell on a reality that she had no hope of changing, Iris offered, "You're a pretty amazing lover, yourself, Asad."

He moved over her body, reminding her of the stalking lion he'd been named for. "I would have you beyond amazed."

"What, you want me passed out from pleasure?" she teased.

"It has happened before."

Yes, it had. "Be my guest." She waved languidly with her hand, as if it didn't matter one way or another to her.

But they both knew it did. She'd never been indifferent to him. She never would be, but maybe, just maybe she would learn to move on from him.

"You have a serious expression I do not like," he said with a frown. "You are not thinking of me."

"Of course I'm thinking of you. Who else would I be thinking of while I am in your bed?"

He looked away, telltale color showing on his cut cheekbones. "I used to wonder."

"What? Why?"

"You were not a virgin when you came to my bed the first time." He met her eyes then. "I thought it mattered."

Yes, he had, though she hadn't known it. "If I recall correctly, it was *my* bed we used the first time, and I was as close to a virgin as you can get."

"What do you mean?"

"Did you think I'd had a string of lovers before you?"

"I preferred not to know details."

Arrogant, possessive sheikh. Even though he'd had no intention of staying with her, he didn't like to think of anyone else with her, either. He didn't deserve the truth, but maybe she deserved for him to know it.

Six years before, she'd thought her innocence obvious and had only learned otherwise when they broke up.

"I lost my virginity on a bet."

"That is…a bet…" For the first time ever, she saw Asad bin Hanif al Sha'b Al'najid lost for words.

It made her smile despite the topic under discussion. "For my high school years, my parents placed me in a coed boarding school known for its science programs."

At least they'd cared enough to take the advice of her middle school counselor on that.

"Yes?"

"There were the typical geeks and jocks, though most of the athletically gifted were highly intelligent, as well. It wasn't easy to get placement in the school and required high marks on the standardized tests."

"I imagine you did very well indeed."

She had, but book smart didn't equal people smart as she'd learned unequivocally her sophomore year. "I was the bookish, shy student who didn't make friends easily."

"Because you were afraid to let them in."

"Partly." And partly because she was socially awkward.

He gently tipped her head back toward him. "I would have been your friend."

It was a nice thing to say, but she couldn't stifle her laughter. "No, you wouldn't. You would have been one of the popular people. You couldn't have helped yourself. You wouldn't have even noticed me."

"I noticed you in college and you had not appreciably changed by then I think."

"True." Why was she sharing her past again when

he wasn't going to be in her future? "Are you sure you want to hear this? It's old news anyway."

"Tell me about this bet."

"The year I was a sophomore, the senior boys had a bet going on for who could bag the most virgins."

"Bag?"

"Get in the sack…have sex with."

"I see, and clearly at that age, you were a virgin."

"I was. When the senior boy who decided to make me one of his conquests started flirting with me, I had no clue what was going on. It was only the middle of the school year, but by then, most of the students knew about the bet, so girls were wary of these boys."

"But you are not a gossip and you pay little attention when it goes on around you."

"Right. So I didn't know. It wouldn't have mattered anyway. I thought he just wanted to be my friend. And the funny thing? We ended up enjoying each other's company a lot. He became my best friend."

Asad winced. "Then you had sex."

"Yes. Despite my naïveté, I wasn't an easy mark— simply because the idea he'd want sex with me was so completely outside my thought process."

"And sex would have been an intimate encounter for you, something you'd already learned to avoid."

"You understand me so well." She bit her lip. "So did Darren. We finally had sex the week before graduation. It only happened once. I didn't like it very much."

"He was harsh?"

"No. He tried to make it good for me. He kept asking me if I was okay. He wasn't a cruel boy, not really. But it was my first time and I wasn't doing it because I wanted him. I never desired anyone that way until I met you. I just wanted to be close to him."

"What a little bastard."

"No. Selfish and thoughtless? Yes." She shrugged. "I didn't know about the bet until two days later when one of the other boys in the competition came up to me and complained about how he'd had it in the bag until I won it for Darren."

"The little prick."

"Yes, *he* was. He wanted me to hurt, to know the sex hadn't been about love, but in that, the joke was on him. I never thought Darren loved me." She'd thought he was her friend and she'd felt enough betrayal from that, though they'd worked through it in the end.

"Yet you had sex with him."

"He was leaving."

"So you gave him your virginity?"

"I don't expect you to understand." Darren had, though. He'd known how hurt she was by the bet too, even though she'd pretended indifference. "Darren's guilt was way worse than my embarrassment."

"Don't tell me you forgave him?"

"He's one of my dearest friends." Though they hadn't seen each other more than a handful of times in the intervening years, they stayed in touch with email and telephone.

He'd invited her to his wedding and introduced Iris to his wife as the girl who had made him the man he'd come to be. That bet had had a transforming influence on Darren, changing forever the way he related to others and decimating the power of peer pressure in his life.

He'd told her once that she'd freed him. She'd told him he was an idiot, but knew deep down that in a way he was right. Only it had been his own deep regret at hurting her and the other girls that had truly set him free.

"You cannot be serious."

"I can. Darren learned not to use people." Iris hadn't been so lucky. She hadn't learned not to be used, not then anyway.

"You cannot be this disgusting boy's friend. I forbid it."

She laughed, finding the telling easier than she'd expected it to be. "Too late. And he's no longer a boy. He's an adult man, married with two children and working in the diplomatic corps."

"I will see about that."

"You will do no such thing. Darren hurt me, but he didn't abandon me, not like you did. The boy who told me about the bet? Darren disowned their friendship."

"He was quite the tarnished knight," Asad said with heavy sarcasm.

"He apologized. We moved forward."

"I too apologized."

"And I'm lying here in your bed. What more do you want, Asad?"

CHAPTER NINE

THE question took Asad by surprise. Surely she knew exactly what he needed from her. "Your forgiveness."

She stared up at him in silence for several long seconds, her captivating blue eyes weighing him in a way he rarely encountered and then said, "I forgive you."

Could it truly be that easy? "You don't mean that."

"Would I be here if I didn't?" she asked, again referring to her place in his bed, their naked bodies pressed together, her gorgeous red tresses spread over his sheets.

"You forgive too easily."

"Not really."

"Yes." And why he should chide her about that when he was benefitting, he did not know.

"Are you saying you want me to go back to ignoring you?"

"No." He wanted her to trust him and somehow he knew her forgiveness did not come packaged with that commodity. "I want you to take me into your body."

It wasn't all he wanted, but since he wasn't sure what exactly that did entail, he didn't try to enlighten her.

Her answer was to shift under him, opening herself to him, but there was a part of herself she held back, a shadow in her eyes that had never been there in the past. Probably inevitable considering their history, but Asad did not have to like it.

Her trust was no longer on offer. And only now did he realize it had been a gift he'd taken every bit of as much for granted as that stupid high school boy had done. But Asad had been old enough to know better.

He would make up for it and he would regain that part of their friendship that he had found so comforting, but had been too blind to see the importance of, six years ago.

If she could forgive the little prick who had taken her virginity, call *him* friend and mean it, she could learn to give true forgiveness to Asad.

Asad reached for a condom. It was time to join their bodies in a way she could not hide from, could not pretend did not matter. Not his Iris.

He had brought her to the pinnacle of pleasure twice already because he knew he would not last long. Asad had only known his own hand for sexual release since well before Badra's death. It was not enough, especially now that he had Iris in touching distance again.

The idea of taking another lover, one that might betray him, or even worse, his daughter, had been anathema to him. Nawar's needs had to come first. Leaving her in order to enjoy liaisons to slake his physical hungers had not appealed to Asad.

He guided his head to Iris's soft opening, pressing forward into the heated honey depths he could never forget, no matter how hard he tried. Her body encased him in pure pleasure and he had the undeniable sensation of coming home.

This was where he belonged. For now, anyway.

Iris gasped as his body claimed hers and he kissed the sound right from her lips.

The baffling sense of coming home was so strong, once he was seated fully, he could not move. Despite the need clamoring in his body for release, he remained still, savoring the sensations that came from amazing sex.

"I will not abandon you again," he promised with the full force of his Bedouin honor. "I will be your best and truest friend."

"Possessive."

"I am."

"You always were."

He could not deny it.

Her voice was strained when she asked, "Are you going to move, Asad?"

"You wish for me to do so?" he taunted.

The clenching of her inner body was his only answer, but her eyes demanded he listen.

So he did, making love to her with less finesse than need. And instead of being bothered by his loss of control, he reveled in it. This was what had been missing for so long in his sex life.

Primitive, ungovernable passion.

In this, Asad's Bedouin heritage ruled, not the urbanity Badra had demanded.

His pleasure built like a volcano inside him, his balls burning with the need to erupt. He gritted his teeth, holding off the explosion as he did his best to bring his *aziz* to climax one more time.

Their mouths joined in a primal echo of what their bodies were doing, sweat slickening the skin between them as he thrust into her.

He felt her climax like it was his own and pleasure boiled up out of his cock with all the power of Mt. Vesuvius.

He shouted his triumph even as she continued to convulse around him.

He broke the kiss, still buried deep inside her. "You are mine."

"Your possessive side is showing again," she gasped out, not sounding like it bothered her in the least.

"I am a sheikh. What do you expect?"

She smiled up at him, her eyes filled with sleepy satiation. "Nothing but what you are. I promise, Asad."

He nodded, knowing her further assurances that she understood the parameters of their relationship fully this time around should please him. But a tiny, primitive part of him did not like it and he was not at all certain why. However, the knowledge that she had no hidden agenda and was not trying to get anything out of him with her capitulation into his bed did something in the region of his heart he would have thought impossible.

It moved him when he had been certain his diamond-hard heart could not be moved.

Carefully withdrawing from her body, he rolled to the side and disposed of the condom. Then he pulled her close so she was completely wrapped in him. Despite the niggle of worry at his response to their lovemaking, for the first time in more years than he cared to count, Asad fell asleep feeling replete.

He woke hours later to Iris trying to leave his bed. She'd pushed his arm off her and was trying to scoot away from him without making a sound.

He slipped his hand back over her stomach, tightening his hold on her. "Where are you going?"

"Back to my room."

"No, *az*—" He broke off before saying the word she'd denied him. "Little flower, you belong here."

"I don't, Asad."

"You do." And he set about proving it to her, claiming her with his body and words until she was sobbing her pleasure out in his arms.

Afterward, they slept again, but he woke her in the early hours of the morning.

She blinked up at him with question. "Time for me to go back to my bed?"

No, damn it. If he had his way, she would not sleep another minute in that tiny bed. "Time for a bath."

"But…"

"Come with me."

He led her to the cave his grandfather had never revealed to the rest of the encampment, the place Hanif had only shown to Asad after his marriage to Badra. The private bathing cavern for the lion of the Sha'b Al'najid.

Carrying a high-powered flashlight, Asad led Iris through a complicated series of passages in the caves beyond the chambers for male and female communal bathing. Whenever they came to a fork, he took the one marked with a peacock feather carved in the rock.

He stopped in a rounded cavern. "This is the personal bathing chamber for my family."

"Nawar didn't mention it." Neither had Genevieve.

It didn't surprise her that the sheikh and his family had their own bathing chambers, but there seemed to be an air of secrecy about it.

"Nawar will not be told of this place until she marries and only if she remains with our tribe after the wedding."

Wow, okay. So, definitely a secret. "What about the rest of your family?"

Asad flipped a switch and soft golden light filled the space. "Only my grandparents and parents are aware of its existence. This was my grandfather's true gift to my grandmother upon their wedding, his way of giving her something to make up for all that she left behind."

Iris gasped, unable to believe what her eyes told her she was seeing. "How?"

"In the beginning, Grandfather used real torches to light the space, but I had a solar lighting system installed."

She hadn't meant the lighting, but that was pretty cool, too. It was the rest of the space that had her so amazed.

"How did he have the tiling done?" she asked in awe as she took in the cave that had been made to look like a five-star European spa.

The single hot-tub-size pool in the center had a mosaic tiled surround wide enough to sit on comfortably and dangle one's feet in the steaming water. An ornate wrought iron handrail led into the water, implying steps had been added inside the natural pool.

The cave walls had been smoothed and tiled with another mosaic of Eastern colors and design, a giant peacock centered on the wall opposite the cavern opening. Ornate marble benches graced the area between the wall and two sides of the pool. And on either side of the opening, there were six-feet-high wrought iron shelving units stocked with fluffy Turkish towels, robes and every bathing necessity and luxury Iris could have imagined.

And even some she wouldn't have.

There was even a fully tiled oversize shower stall off to one side. With no door, or curtain, it was clearly intended to be used in luxurious privacy.

"How...the shower...it's not possible."

Asad smiled, pride gleaming in his espresso gaze. "For a Bedouin man with an engineering degree, such things are possible indeed."

"Your grandfather has a degree in engineering?" she asked, feeling more and more like Alice having dropped through the rabbit hole.

Asad nodded. "I told you he'd gone to university in Europe. Many of the modern improvements in our camp are of Grandfather's making."

"He is an amazing man." Just like his grandson.

"He is."

"He acts like he knows only the way of the desert tradition."

"Because at heart, he is that man, but he is more than that, as well."

"Just as you are."

"Yes."

"Thank you for bringing me here." She didn't really understand why Asad had decided to share his family's private oasis with her, but it touched her that he had.

He shrugged, looked pained and then said, "It is what a dear and truest friend would do."

"Ah, so you're still lobbying for that position."

"It would seem I am," he said, sounding a little surprised by that fact himself.

She smiled, not minding in the least. Not when it had such results. She was a woman like any other in this respect...she wasn't about to turn down the opportunity for a bit of pampering.

"It's really wonderful," she said, letting her appreciation of both his grandfather's and Asad's achievements show in her voice.

"It is indeed." He placed his hands on her shoulders,

his expression turning carnal. "Shall we take advantage of the amenities?"

"Yes. Definitely, yes." Dropping her bag with the clean clothes she'd thought she would don after bathing in the communal chamber, she stripped quickly.

She'd never been shy around him, not even in the beginning. Which had always confused her. She'd thought it meant he was the one for her; now she knew he simply brought out the wanton no other man would probably ever meet.

"Beautiful," he said in a husky tone she knew well.

She spun to face him, not in the least surprised to find him watching her. He'd used to watch her all the time, and not just when she was naked. He liked to watch her sleep, to work, to read, to study…doing just about anything.

It used to charm her; she realized it still did. "You like what you see?"

"You know I do."

"Maybe I need you to show me again." She ruthlessly pressed down the guilt at the prospect of getting a late start on her day.

Because with that look in Asad's dark gaze, she knew the last thing she was in for was a quickie.

But Sheikh Hakim had been fine with her taking a full day off simply to get welcomed by the Sha'b Al'najid; a few hours more today wasn't going to make a huge difference in how quickly she got her survey and reports done.

That was her story anyway, and she was sticking to it.

"You need more evidence of how very desirable I find you, my little flower?" he asked, his hands reaching out to tease at her breasts, caress her belly and then dip between her legs.

She moaned, letting her head fall back and just enjoyed his touch for several pleasure-filled moments.

Then she began undressing him, a small tremor of desire in her fingers. "Define need."

All humor drained from his features, leaving a look of such intensity it took her breath away. "What I feel for you."

"Asad…" She tipped her head back again, this time offering her lips.

With a strangled sound he yanked her toward him and took her mouth in a searing kiss. He swept his tongue inside, dueling with hers, tasting her, letting her taste him.

After a night filled with lovemaking, he kissed her as if he had been starved for it.

Needing to feel his naked skin against hers, she scrabbled at his *thobe,* yanking the traditional garment up and over his head, whimpering when that meant breaking their kiss, and going right back to it when the material was out of the way.

She twined her hands behind his neck, pressing her body against his, her already-excited nipples, tender from all his ministrations the night before rubbing against the silky curls on his chest.

She moaned in pleasure at this caress that had always been one of her favorites. Though she liked it even better with his chest hair left to grow naturally. There was just something so wild about her body taking pleasure from his and knowing how much he liked her to do so. Knowing that he was getting every bit as turned on as she was, the need between them growing like an out-of-control tornado.

His hands moved down her body with swift, sure movements to cup her bottom, and then he lifted her so his already-hardened flesh brushed against the apex of her thighs.

Needy sounds filled the steamy air around them, so like six years ago and yet so different. He was stronger now. His reactions were even more primal than they used to be, as if he'd stopped attempting to rein himself in. And she loved that.

She was more aware of what the world of sex had to offer and…not to offer. Innocent embarrassment at her own desires was a thing of the past. She knew how magical this was now, how much she would miss it when it was gone—so she reveled in every second, every breath and touch.

Even the hunger between them was both familiar and altogether different. It was so much stronger now, though she never would have believed that possible. Her craving for him was an ache inside her, but his want was out there for both of them to see and wholly undeniable. He had made love to her short hours before, but the urgency in his touch was as if they had yet to reach their first orgasm.

She felt movement and then her back against the cool tile of the wall. His grip shifted so that he had her thighs over his forearms, her legs spread, her sex open to him.

He pressed against her, but waited as if asking if this was what she wanted. She tilted her hips and pressed down, taking the tip of his engorged sex inside stretched and swollen tissues unused to so much activity.

It didn't hurt; she was experiencing too much plea-sure for that, but she felt it. Felt her body stretch to accommodate him, felt the slide of his hard-on against her inner walls, filling her in a way only he could do.

He tilted her just enough so that his head rubbed against her G-spot on both the pull and push of every thrust of his hips.

Ecstasy built inside her one electric jolt at a time until she was writhing against him as he possessed her. She couldn't think, could barely breathe. It was too much and not enough.

He knew. He always knew.

He swiveled his hips, grinding against her sweet spot with his pelvic bone and she shattered. She was barely aware as he shouted out his own release, his hot essence filling her core.

And if a ridiculous wish that she didn't have the uterine insert played through her mind, no one else ever need know.

She'd given up her dreams of babies and her own family when he'd walked out of her life six years ago. So, the dream wasn't quite as dead as she believed. That was a weakness she would forgive herself.

They stayed like that, connected against the wall, for several long moments, the only sound their harsh breathing. Eventually, he made noise that could have been approval or something else, she was too out of it herself to really tell.

But it was followed by him carrying her to the shower and she realized the sound might even have been words. They bathed each other with the delicious-smelling soap Genevieve was so partial to.

They were soaking in the hot spring pool when Asad said with all the seriousness and more chagrin than she'd ever witnessed in him, "I forgot the condom."

Only then did she realize she hadn't told him she was covered for birth control.

"Are you clean?" she asked softly, aware that pregnancy wasn't the only thing a modern woman had to worry about when having sex.

She sincerely doubted he was a reckless lover, but he had forgotten the condom when he didn't realize she could not get pregnant.

He stared at her in confusion for several seconds before understanding dawned in his brown gaze and he growled, "I am not diseased."

"I'm not trying to offend you. It was a legitimate question."

"So you say. I say we have a much more serious worry to consider here."

"No, we don't."

"You are on the pill?" He looked astonished by the idea.

She wasn't about to be offended by that. She didn't date. Her last sex had been with him; she hadn't been willing to trust anyone else with the intimacy since. "No. I have a uterine insert."

"Why?"

"Do we really have to talk about this?"

"Yes. I want to know." He sure didn't sound like it, though.

"You couldn't be like other men and just pretend this part of my life is a great mystery, could you?" she asked hopefully.

"No," he practically snarled.

"Don't get mad." He was such a caveman sometimes. "It's not a big deal. I just had difficult periods and wanted to do something about it. My doctor suggested the insert, and I don't have any bleeding at all now. It's a huge relief, considering how much time I spend in the field and a lot of it in more primitive conditions than this."

She was sure that was more than he ever wanted to know, but she got a perverse pleasure in giving him the gritty details. After all, he was the one who insisted on knowing and got all cranky when she'd hesitated telling him.

"Will it affect your ability to have children?"

"I doubt I'll ever be a mother, but not because I won't be capable of getting pregnant. There's no risk of infertility." She frowned at him, letting him know that this was not her favorite topic of conversation. "Can we be done with this conversation now?"

"Yes." He looked far too complacent.

Maybe that explained what popped out of her mouth next. "Did you bring Badra here?" she asked, realizing almost immediately how much she wanted to bite her own tongue off.

First, because of course he'd brought Badra here; the princess had been his wife. And second, because Iris *really* didn't want to know about it. Not even a little.

Idiot.

"No."

"What?" *No?*

"My grandfather showed me this place on the eve of my wedding, but Badra insisted on being married in her father's palace."

"Wouldn't that be traditional?" And why would it prevent Asad from bringing his wife to the private bathing chamber when they returned to his city of tents?

"Not for a sheikh of my people. Even my parents were married here."

"Oh, but she wanted to get married with the traditions of her family?" That was understandable.

"She wanted to put off joining the encampment for as long as possible, though I did not realize it at the time. She'd convinced me to take her on a tour of Europe for our honeymoon."

"Um, sounds special?" Iris's comment came out more a question than a statement because he sounded so disdainful of their honeymoon plans.

"Our tradition would have dictated I take her into the desert for a time of privacy and bonding. She refused."

"So she wasn't much of a camper."

"She was a poor wife and even worse Bedouin. Badra was not a virgin on our wedding night."

CHAPTER TEN

"THAT must have been a shock to you." A really unpleasant one, too.

Remembering back to their breakup, she knew how important sexual innocence had been to Asad. Probably still was. Iris hadn't realized it when they were dating, but when he told her it was over he'd made a lot of things clear that had been hazy before that. Like the fact that Iris could never be in the running for Asad's future wife because she'd had a sexual partner before him.

Even now, with their friendship firmly intact, she couldn't think of Darren as a former lover. There had been no love in the loss of her virginity. Not even on her part.

Iris had thought Asad's attitude pretty much prehistoric, but her opinion hadn't counted. And he'd walked away to marry the not-so-perfect Badra.

"She was also pregnant."

"What? Nawar isn't yours?" Iris asked in shock.

But there was no doubting the bond between the beautiful little girl and her father.

"She is mine," Asad fiercely contradicted. "Though she carries none of my genetic makeup, Nawar is in all ways that count my beloved daughter."

"But that's…" Unbelievable.

Or kind of funny in a gallows-humor kind of way. Not that his daughter didn't share his gene pool, but because of the way he'd rejected Iris so completely based on her lack of innocence. Only, Iris had been way more virginal in the ways that counted than the already-pregnant Badra. That was for sure.

But mostly, the whole situation with Badra seemed really, really sad. She'd deceived Asad and Nawar had been made a pawn in a marriage paved with bad intention before she'd ever been born.

"I'm sorry." Iris really, really was.

"Do not be. The one good thing I got out of my marriage to Badra was my precious gem, Nawar."

Iris liked hearing that; it gave her confidence that under the more cynical and dour exterior, Asad was still the same man who had once really been her best and truest friend. His willingness to share what had to be his deepest secret with her showed that regardless of the intervening years of silence, he still saw her in that light.

"Nawar said you named her."

"Badra had no interest in parenting from the very beginning. Though at the time, I believed she allowed me to name Nawar to make her more my own. I was wrong about that, just as I had mistaken so much about Badra. At first I believed Badra's lack of interest in my daughter was due to her shame at bearing another man's child. I told her repeatedly how much I loved Nawar. That I did not resent her."

"That's kind of amazing." And so not what Iris would have expected of the arrogant, proud man.

She'd loved Asad, but she hadn't been blind to his faults. Or so she had believed. Perhaps she'd been blinder to more things than even their subsequent break-up had forced her to accept.

"I was not there for the birth, as is the custom of our people, but my grandmother brought the babe to me when she was less than an hour old. I looked down into her beautiful little face and fell in love."

Emotion caught in Iris's throat. "She's very lucky to have you for a father."

"I am far more blessed to have her as a daughter."

Iris thought maybe it was a draw, but forbore saying so.

"I named her flower after the one woman I knew had more honor than my wife ever would."

The import of Asad's words finally registered and Iris gasped in shock. "You named your daughter after me. That's not possible."

"I assure you, it is. Though at the time I was unaware of what my brain had done. I only realized it later, but then so did Badra. When she did, it infuriated her. We fought about it and rather than deny it like I should have because I was totally unaware of having done it, I told Badra I wanted Nawar to share your sense of honor, not her mother's."

"That's..." Iris didn't know what to say. How did you answer a statement like that? "I guess I'm glad to know you think I have strong character."

"I do, very much so. It made you a good friend and trustworthy lover."

There was no denying his words. The trust he was showing in her now matched what she had given him the night before, when she'd shared her past shame with him. It came to Iris then that Asad had not realized what he would lose when he dumped her, or how much he would miss her. Another tiny bit of her shattered heart mended at that knowledge.

"Unless I want a distant cousin to take my place, I will have to marry again."

Well, that came out of the blue and frankly, Iris could have lived without that reminder. Nevertheless, she said, "Yes." And then the import of what he'd said hit her. "Badra intended to stick you with another man's child. What if Nawar had been a boy?"

"He would have been the next sheikh of my people. Nawar's husband may well be my successor."

Iris believed him. And again...wow. This man was everything she'd believed him to be and then convinced herself he wasn't, and so much more.

Asad loved his daughter, and he would have loved a son just as well. That was the kind of man he was. Asad had honor and character to spare. Even if at one time she'd maybe thought he didn't.

"So Badra told you she was pregnant?"

"Only after I figured it out for myself, the day after our wedding."

Their honeymoon must have been a treat, Iris thought rather sarcastically and then felt bad for thinking at all. Poor Asad.

"Whoever I marry must accept Nawar as completely as I do."

"Of course."

He smiled, as if happy with her answer. The man did have a rather well-developed need, or maybe expectation, that the people around him would agree with his opinion. Not that he was great at compromise, or anything. He just liked knowing everyone thought he was right.

Arrogant sheikh. She smiled.

"What is that expression on your face?"

"I'm smiling."

"I am aware."

"That's not exactly a rare occurrence."

"Less common than I remember from six years ago."

"I could say the same."

He shrugged and then pulled her into his arms through the water. "The responsibilities of my position have tempered my humor."

And maybe learning his perfect princess was anything but had robbed Asad of some of his joy in life. Not that Iris expected him to ever admit it.

She let herself relax against him, enjoying this intimacy almost as much as what they'd shared earlier. "You said that Badra died in a plane crash with her lover. Did she leave you?"

"No. She traveled with him several times a year."

"And you put up with it?" Iris asked in shock, turning around to face him, water sloshing over the sides of the pool from her agitated movements.

"I had full control of Nawar's raising. This was the important thing. Badra signed away parental rights to my daughter in exchange for five years of me funding her lifestyle and accepting her choices therein."

"Five years?" Iris asked faintly.

"Yes. I would have divorced Badra a year ago if she were not already dead."

"But that's medieval."

"It was necessary. She could have taken my daughter and I could not allow it."

So he'd bought rights to her daughter. "There were other ways." There had to have been.

"None that guaranteed Nawar, my little jewel, stayed

with me here among the Sha'b Al'najid whom she loved and who loved her just as fiercely."

"So you gave up five years of your life for her." He really was the most amazing man ever.

"I was prepared to, yes."

"You're a Superman, you know that?"

"I am glad you think so, but you did not believe this six years ago."

"Oh, I did. Just not after you dumped me." She took a deep breath and let it out. "But that's in the past. I don't want to talk, or even think about it anymore. Okay?"

"As you wish. The present is enough to keep us both fully occupied."

She believed he was right about that.

"You slept with him," Russell whispered in cheeky accusation as they completed their first set of measurements at the initial sampling site.

Iris's head snapped around. "Shhh…I don't know why you'd say that anyway."

She wasn't going to deny it. Iris was a terrible liar, but admitting she was sleeping with the man who'd broken her heart once wasn't going to make her look all that smart to her colleague.

"Give it a rest, cupcake. It's all there in his eyes."

"What's in his eyes?" she couldn't help asking, though she knew she shouldn't.

The look on Russell's face said he knew he'd gotten her. "At the palace, and since, he's watched you with this really intense yearning." He frowned, sadness entering his gaze. "It's an expression I understand too well not to recognize."

Iris reached out and squeezed his arm in silent comfort. Russell's ex-girlfriend had really done a number on him. And knowing how deeply Asad's defection had affected her, Iris wasn't about to dismiss Russell's love affair gone wrong as a youthful mistake he would get over easily.

"He's not looking at you like that now, though," Russell claimed, his voice cheerful, the look of sadness gone.

She waited several seconds for her nosy colleague to explain, but he just went back to work. Finally, in exasperation, she asked, "How does he look at, then?"

"Like you're his and anyone thinking to challenge that claim had better protect his balls."

She burst out laughing, but the man who wore T-shirts with humorous sayings only another geologist would really appreciate—today's said Don't Take Me For Granite, Just Because I'm Gneiss—looked as serious as bedrock. "I think you better watch out for your heart, Iris."

That was one warning she didn't need. She already knew how hazardous Asad was to her heart.

"What's so funny?" Nawar asked, skipping up to join them, her father only a few steps behind.

Iris had worried that having them along would make doing her job difficult, but Asad was good with his daughter and this mountainous desert was his homeland. They'd kept busy with an impromptu lesson on geography targeted at the four-year-old's level. Iris had no idea how much the child would remember, but something told her it would be more than she might expect.

"Russell made me laugh," Iris said with a smile for the little girl.

Asad's brows rose, his expression this side of dangerous. "Oh?"

"Told you," Russell mouthed, his head facing Iris and away from Asad.

Iris shook her head.

"He did not make you laugh?" Asad asked.

Iris rolled her eyes. "Does it matter? How are you two doing? Bored?"

"Not in the least, but I believe it is time to take a break for eating and then Nawar will have her nap."

"Where?" Surely the SUV would be too warm for the little girl to sleep in.

Though it was not as hot here as the desert at the base of the mountains, it was still sunny enough to heat the interior to uncomfortable levels.

"There." He indicated the other side of the SUV.

And Iris noticed that while she had been working, he'd erected a small single-room goat-hair tent with an awning that created a second area in front open to any light breezes. It said something about how caught up in her work she got that she hadn't even noticed him putting the tent up. Iris had no doubt the portable Bedouin home would be perfectly comfortable for Nawar's nap.

"You're a good dad."

He shrugged. "I did not want you to feel rushed to return to the encampment."

"Thank you."

"You are welcome." His eyes watched her lips.

She swayed forward, but caught herself before kissing him in front of his daughter and Russell. What was she thinking?

Thankfully Nawar caught their attention then, trying to drag the oversize basket of food prepared for them from the tent by herself.

They chatted while they ate and then Asad put his yawning daughter down for her nap. Afterward, he made himself comfortable under the awning with his laptop, the sheikh of the Sha'b Al'najid working on very modern business in an equally old setting.

Russell caught Iris watching Asad and shook his head.

"What?"

"You've got it bad...you do know that?"

"I *had* it bad, six years ago."

"But not now? Wake up and smell the cordite, Iris. The man is so far under your skin, he's got a direct path to your heart." Russell set the core sampler in the ground.

"No," she said more loudly than she intended. "I'm not going to love him again."

"You're trying to say you ever stopped?"

She glared at Russell, who blithely ignored her while he drew a clean sample of topsoil. "Enough of the personal observations. We've got plenty to do here without you turning into Dr. Phil on me."

"Hey, I resent that." He flicked her a grin over his shoulder. "I've got all my hair."

"You've got a big mouth is what you've got."

He stopped what he was doing and really looked at her, his expression back to the unfamiliar seriousness. "I'm your friend, Iris. I'm not going to lie to you."

"Your truth isn't necessarily my truth."

"Oh, very Zen of you." He was back to being a smart aleck.

"Stop, or I'm going to tell Genevieve you want grasshoppers in your dinner."

"That lady sure does like you. It's almost as if she's looking forward to you joining the family," he said meaningfully.

"Russell," she practically yelled. One thing Iris

could not afford was to allow Russell to plant ideas in her head that would only get her heart shattered a second time around.

"Fine, fine…I'll stop."

Despite their late start, Iris and Russell gathered a good day's worth of samples, measurement and observations. Preliminary indications made her think that mining might very well be in Kadar's future.

But Iris didn't say anything of that nature to Asad or his family over dinner when they asked how her first day on the job had gone. Russell was dining with another family, getting the opportunity to experience more elements of the Bedouin culture.

Iris did not complain about not being afforded the same opportunity. There was nowhere she'd rather be and that was her personal cross to bear. Certainly, she didn't need Russell's observations on the matter.

Iris snuggled against Asad, their early-morning lovemaking having left her feeling drowsy and relaxed. "Are you coming with us again today?"

"But of course. I told you I would be your guide and protector while you are here."

"How can you afford the time?" Challenging enough to be a business mogul, or a sheikh, but to be both?

She doubted many men could handle the pressure.

"I will bring my computer and do work as I did yesterday."

"You spent a good portion of yesterday keeping Nawar occupied."

"She is my joy."

"She is incredibly sweet, but that doesn't answer my question."

"What question is that, *az*—Iris?"

She noticed him stumbling over the old endearment again, but pretended not to. "How you can have the time to babysit Russell and me like this? You can send someone else if you really feel we need looking after. It doesn't have to be you."

"Excuse me, but it does."

"Come on, Asad. You've got what you want. You don't need to keep playing nursemaid."

"And what is it you believe I want?" he asked.

She rolled her eyes, though he wouldn't see it with her head pillowed on his shoulder. Like he thought she wouldn't know. "Me. *Here.*"

"I do want that, but there is more I desire, as well."

"What?"

"Your safety, for one."

"Seriously?" She sat up and stared down at Asad. "You don't really think Russell and I are at any risk in the field. Kadar is not exactly a hotbed of crime. And the desert even less so."

"Not all who come to these mountains are as honorable as the Sha'b Al'najid."

"And Russell and I aren't exactly doing our survey in the path of most travelers." They were in foothills of the desert mountains, hours from the nearest village, twice as far from anything resembling a town or city.

"Who do you think knows of the two Western geologists doing their survey here in Kadar?"

"The sheikh and your family. I doubt even the whole camp knows why Russell and I are here." They just weren't that interesting.

Asad got up from the bed and drew on his thobe. "You would be wrong. Every member of my people knows of your purpose and the way you spend your days. Be assured many others do, as well. Gossip travels among the Bedouin like the sand in a storm in the desert."

"So?"

"All who have heard this juicy tidbit of news are not so scrupulous as you would like to believe. The least dangerous are those that might merely covet your equipment for the money it could bring them." He tossed her a hooded robe that swallowed her up when she put it on.

Meant to hit him midcalf, it brushed the carpet on her.

"Who is the most dangerous?" she asked, finding it difficult to keep her amusement at his paranoid worries hidden.

"Slavers."

"Oh, please." Now he was really reaching.

"Modern slavery is a nine-billion-dollar-a-year industry and a worldwide problem."

"But the crime rate in Kadar is almost nonexistent."

"There are always exceptions." He frowned. "You will not be one of them."

"If you're so worried about it, then I'm surprised you're willing to bring Nawar."

He slid traditional leather slippers onto his feet. "You do not imagine that we travel into the mountains alone."

"We did yesterday."

"Did we?"

"Yes?"

"No. My guards are well trained and maintain their distance to give us the illusion of privacy."

"You're not joking."

"Why would I make light of something so important?"

Why indeed, but the idea of having men lurking in

the shadows and watching her was kind of creepy. "So you're saying we've got a troupe of Ninjas hiding in plain sight protecting us?"

"Not Ninja, warriors of the Sha'b Al'najid."

"You still have warriors in your tribe?" she asked with keen interest, her discomfort pushed aside in favor of feeding her curiosity.

"Every man is trained in the ways of stealth, fighting and the scimitar. It is tradition among my people. There is an elite force, my family's bodyguards, that are trained in the ways of modern warfare, as well."

"Your tribe is a lot wealthier than anyone would guess, aren't they?"

"My family is."

"But your family accepts responsibility for the Sha'b Al'najid."

"Yes."

"Amazing."

"It is what it is."

"Badra was such an idiot."

"You think so?" Asad stopped in front of Iris, looking down at her with surprising intensity.

"I do." Iris reached up and traced his lips, smiling when he nipped at her fingertip. "She had you and all of this and still, she wanted something else."

He leaned down and kissed her, not passionately, but not chastely, either. It was intimate and gentle and quick...and it felt really nice. "I am flattered you feel that way."

Iris wished she could share his equanimity about it. She was beginning to have some serious reservations about her current course of action. Yes, her heart was healing bit by bit, but was it just going to shatter again into a million pieces when she left Kadar?

She'd thought she could keep love out of the equation, but a mere two nights in his bed and Iris was already grasping for a lifeline while she felt herself drowning in dormant emotions.

"It would be a lot easier for me if you could simply act like the selfish user I convinced myself you were after you dumped me," she complained with more honesty than she probably should have offered.

But he didn't look like he minded, his dark eyes glowing. "You no longer see me as this person?"

She shrugged, the effect lost under the voluminous folds of his robe on her.

"Iris?" he prompted.

She sighed and admitted, "I'm learning that neither of our perceptions of the past was all that clear."

"You are right. I thought you were far more experienced—"

Her snort of disbelief interrupted him.

"What?"

"How could you not realize how inexperienced I was back then? I was terrified you would get bored with my lack of prowess and go looking for greener pastures."

"The passion between us was always so fiery—there was no room for practiced moves. I assumed you were as overwhelmed by desire as I was."

"I was."

"Yes, but with less experience."

"Bragging now, are you?"

"Never. I have no need to brag. You think I am the most amazing lover ever."

"Conceited."

"Deny it."

"You know I won't."

"Can't," he charged with one raised eyebrow.

She huffed fondly, "Jerk."

"Is that the proper endearment to use for the man who rocks your world?"

"And what of the woman who rocks yours?" she asked facetiously.

"You will not allow me the proper endearment," he accused.

"Poor you."

He shook his head. "You are still determined I should not call you *aziz?*"

"Very." That was one thing she was still absolutely sure about. Though her other beliefs and feelings were in something of a muddle, she knew she didn't want him using the term for beloved when she wasn't.

"One day you will allow it."

"I won't be in Kadar long enough for that to happen." Considering the area Sheikh Hakim had hired her company to survey, Iris would be in Kadar only a month, six weeks at the outside.

It could have been a much more involved study, but Sheikh Hakim had ordered only a first-level survey. Most likely because he would use it to determine which areas to pursue further.

Nevertheless, Asad, did not look like he believed Iris's claim. "Come with me to the baths and I will see what I can do about changing your mind."

CHAPTER ELEVEN

For the next two weeks, the days followed the pattern set on that one.

Asad and Nawar accompanied Iris and Russell to their survey sites. Against all expectations, Iris had never enjoyed her job more and found it surprisingly easy to accomplish what she needed to, despite their presence. And that of the unseen guards who joined them every day.

Both she and Russell couldn't help taking time to show the curious little girl how they used their portable geological equipment. And somehow there was always time for play, as well.

Iris found herself falling for the child every bit as heavily as she'd fallen for the father. Her wish that she had been Nawar's mother grew daily, but she kept it hidden. It was dangerous, but Iris allowed herself to wallow in what it would feel like to be a real family.

She thought sometimes that Nawar was doing the same thing, and that both delighted and frightened her. She didn't want Asad's daughter hurt when Iris had to leave.

Iris was currently showing Nawar how to identify a rock, Asad having asked her to watch Nawar while he took a call on his satellite phone. "The first thing we look at is color. What color would you say this is?"

"Brown." Nawar squinted at the rock, as if determining the correctness of her answer.

Iris hid her grin and nodded as solemnly as she could. "Very good. Now feel the rock—is it smooth or rough?"

"It's bumpy."

This time Iris let herself smile. "Right. We can do a test on the rock to see what kind of minerals are in it to get a proper identification."

"What's a min-rall?"

Russell laughed, showing he had been listening.

Iris smiled a little sheepishly. "Minerals are things like iron and zinc."

"Like my vitamins?" Nawar asked, proving she was a very intelligent child.

"Yes, exactly like that. Who told you your vitamins had iron and zinc in them?"

"Papa said I need my iron to grow strong."

Iris remembered Asad saying that Nawar didn't care for meat and ate a practically vegetarian diet. Considering the other foods that comprised the Bedouin diet, she thought she understood why he would want his daughter to take a minimal iron supplement in her children's vitamin.

"He's right, of course."

"Oh. I want zinc in my vitamins."

Iris had no idea if children's vitamins had zinc in them. She would have to do some research before making any promises. "I'll talk to your daddy about it. If you need zinc, I'm sure he'll make sure you get it."

"A mommy would make sure, wouldn't she?"

"I…um…I suppose so."

"Papa said I'm going to have a new mommy soon."

"He did?" Iris asked faintly, a band squeezing tightly around her chest, making it hard to breathe.

Nawar nodded solemnly. "He said it was time."

"That's good." The words cost her, but not nearly as much as the even tone Iris used to say them.

"I'm ever so excited." And Nawar looked it, her eyes so like her father's—even if they didn't share the genes to make it so—glowing brightly with happiness at the thought. "He said I would like her very much."

"I'm glad."

"Me, too. Grandmother says Papa is lonely. My mommy will be his wife."

Oh, gosh, she was going to be sick. "Yes, I do believe that's how it works."

"Do you think she'll be a princess like my other mother?"

"I don't know."

"I don't care. She doesn't have to be a princess." Nawar gave Iris a look she had no hope of understanding.

Not in her current state. It was taking everything she had to remain pleasant and smiling with the little girl so blithely shredding hopes she'd been so sure she hadn't let herself entertain once again.

Badra wasn't the idiot; Iris was.

"I'm sure whoever she is, she'll be a very good mommy," Iris said softly.

"Yes. She'll like me and want to spend time with me." Nawar was back to looking too serious for her years. "Papa promised."

"He loves you very much."

"I love him. He's the bestest."

"He is a wonderful man." Even if he was making

plans to marry someone else while sharing his bed with Iris. Again.

Iris wanted to curse her own stupidity and Asad's plans in equal measure, but she bit back words not appropriate for little ears.

Russell's expression of concern was not helping. She frowned at him and shook her head, her eyes warning him not to say anything.

Asad hadn't made any promises and she'd gone into this thing with him knowing it had a sell-by date of weeks, not even months. So it was no one's fault but her own that hearing of his plans to marry someone else was ripping her apart inside.

It wasn't supposed to be this way this time. Somehow she had to get a handle on her emotions, but Iris couldn't help her quiet over lunch.

She ignored the looks of question Asad kept sliding in her direction. Doing her best to bring her emotions into line, she determinedly focused on eating and not throwing up.

After they'd packed away the lunch things, Asad put Nawar down for a nap and then asked Iris to take a walk with him.

But she shook her head. She wasn't ready to be alone with him, not yet. "I need to work and so do you."

"Nevertheless, we will go for a walk." The set of his jaw said while he'd phrased the initial offer as a request, they would indeed be going, one way or another.

With pictures of herself dangling over his shoulder as he marched along the path, she reluctantly nodded.

Refusing would only delay the inevitable anyway. Iris couldn't hide her upset at Nawar's news and Asad wasn't about to ignore it.

He offered his hand, but she pretended not to see it.

"We're back to that, are we?" he asked as he led her on a narrow path she had noticed earlier doing some measurements.

Iris wanted to deny it, or simply ignore it, or anything but deal with it, but that wasn't going to happen.

"Nawar tells me that you promised her a new mother soon." And the news should not bother her—she knew it shouldn't.

This time around, she had *known* they had no future. But the hurt was there all the same. This man had always been able to get past her defenses and believing this time would be different had been more than shortsighted of her, it had been criminally stupid.

"Yes."

When he didn't say anything else as they followed the trek through some trees and up the side of the mountain, Iris contemplated demanding answers and/or kicking him in the shin. Neither prospect promised to have an advantageous outcome.

"It's true, then?" she asked regardless.

"It is."

"So this is just like six years ago?"

"No."

She stopped and grabbed his desert robe to halt him, as well. He turned to face her, his inscrutable sheikh face firmly in place.

"How is it different?" she demanded. "You're having sex with me while planning to marry another woman."

For a moment something like pain flared briefly in his espresso gaze. "No."

"No?" Iris asked sarcastically. How could he say that? "You don't have another woman picked out and waiting in the wings to step in as Nawar's mommy?"

As his wife.

"No."

"But…" She did her best to assimilate the meaning of his answers in the face of what Nawar had said.

Asad had promised his daughter a mother. He did not deny it. Yet he hadn't said he knew who that woman was going to be. In fact, if he did, wouldn't Nawar have already met her?

He loved his daughter too much to choose a wife without insuring she was compatible with his daughter.

So the replacement had *not* been chosen. Inexplicably, that knowledge lightened Iris's heart immeasurably. "I see."

"I sincerely doubt it."

"I'm not stupid."

"Just blind."

She let go of the hold she still had on his sleeve and took a step back. "I stopped being blind six years ago."

"Six years ago I was the blind idiot, not you." He turned and started back on the path.

Feeling uncertain, yet oddly hopeful, she followed him. "Yes, well…we both learned our lessons I guess."

"Did we? I'm beginning to wonder."

"So, where does this path lead?"

"To an overlook popular with shepherds and lovers."

"Um…okay."

They'd been walking in an unexpectedly companionable silence for several minutes when he observed, "It bothered you to think I had plans to marry another woman."

Technically he still did, but she didn't want to get into that discussion. "I would never willingly be *the other woman*."

"No, you have too much integrity for that."

"I was, though, six years ago."

It was his turn to stop their progress. He turned to her, his expression grim. "No, you were not."

"You said—"

"That I had plans to marry Badra, not that she'd accepted my proposal. My plans were not hers, nor were they set in stone, no matter that my will insisted it be so. In fact, the first time I asked her, she told me with great contempt that she would never tie herself to an ignorant goatherd."

That explained his oversensitivity on the topic, but Iris couldn't help feeling pleased at the knowledge she had never truly been cast in the role of mistress.

"You were in line to be sheikh, though."

"Of a Bedouin tribe."

"What difference does that make?"

"I live in a *beit al-sha'r,* the house of hair. Not a palace."

"By choice."

"It was not a choice Badra approved of."

"Even if she hadn't been a cheating abandoner of children, you two would have been a really bad match." Iris hoped Asad could see that now.

He really *had* been every bit as blind as she was six years ago.

"You think she abandoned Nawar?" he asked curiously.

There was no doubt in Iris's mind, or her heart. "Didn't she? Badra signed over parental rights in exchange for a cushy lifestyle and the promise of freedom at the end of five years."

It was only as she said the words that she realized that Asad's parents had done much the same to him.

"You mean like my parents," he said, proving that just like in the past, their brains often traveled down the same paths.

"No. I'm not saying I could or even would have made the choices your parents made, but they kept loving, kept wanting to be part of your life. I get the feeling Badra was a little more like my parents, completely uninterested in having her daughter in her life."

"Nawar is my daughter and you are absolutely right."

"You protected Nawar because you understood what it felt like to have your parents put your interests second," Iris said in sudden understanding on a burst of emotion she didn't want to name.

"I did not consider it in the same light. I always had my grandparents and my place here among the Sha'b Al'najid."

But his parents had traded the right to raise their oldest son in their home for the ability to have that home where and at the level of luxury they wanted it. The desire to reach out and comfort him was too strong to deny and she took his hand.

He said nothing, but his grip on her hand was strong.

They continued their walk in silence, Iris's brain too busy to truly appreciate the beauty around her. She could not stop thinking about the fact that if Asad was not actively looking for his next wife, he would be soon.

Not until after Iris had left Kadar, though…from his attitude she was pretty certain of that.

A small voice in her heart asked why that woman could not be Iris? For once, her usually analytical brain could not give an adequate answer. *Why couldn't she be Nawar's mom and Asad's wife?*

Iris would love Nawar as if she'd given her birth;

she was close to doing so already. There was something about the small girl that Iris identified with, a vulnerability she understood all too well. Iris knew what it was to be abandoned emotionally by a parent; she would never let the little girl experience that pain at her own hands.

Beyond that, their relationship six years ago had proven she and Asad were compatible in and out of bed. They had been best and truest friends. That compatibility was very much in evidence again today. As was their friendship, maybe even a deeper one.

They'd shared things they never would have six years ago, being open in ways that they hadn't been then.

And it felt right and good.

So, why not her?

Iris might not be a snooty Middle Eastern princess, but that was a benefit to her way of thinking. Neither Nawar nor Asad had done so well the first time around with one of those. Genevieve hadn't been either and Asad claimed she'd been the most beloved Lady of the Sha'b Al'najid in generations.

His grandfather certainly didn't seem disappointed in his wife's lack of Middle Eastern heritage or pedigree.

Surely Asad had to realize that a woman who loved him and Nawar would be better than any pedigreed pretender.

And Iris did love him, totally and completely. It was inevitable. Staying out of his bed would not have prevented it, because Russell had been right. There had been no danger of Iris falling in love a second time when she'd never stopped in the first place.

No amount of will could prevail against the depth of feeling she had toward Asad.

This time around, she knew she had to fight for what she wanted, that the possibility of having it taken away again lurked around the next bend in the road.

She had to show him that she would make him a better wife than any other woman ever could, just as he would be the ideal husband for her. He might not realize he loved her, but he couldn't make love to her the way he did and feel nothing.

She'd thought at one time he had done, but now she knew it had cost him to leave her. That he'd never forgotten her. He'd even named his daughter after her. And he'd wanted her back in his bed enough to cajole his cousin into making sure she was the geologist sent for this survey.

Any way Iris looked at it, Asad felt more for her than he realized.

Marrying him might mean Iris giving up her current job, but that didn't mean she couldn't start something new. Living among the Sha'b Al'najid and exploring the world they lived in could take a lifetime for even the most devoted geologist.

Six years ago Asad hadn't considered Iris a candidate to become part of his family, but he'd admitted to having been blind and stupid. He implied he wasn't either any longer.

If that was true, then she had a few short weeks to show her new and improved, open-eyed sheikh the light.

It had taken Iris twenty-four years to give up on fighting for her parents' affection. She could be stubborn and determined with the best of them, even if others rarely saw that side of her.

It was time Asad did, at least.

When they reached the overlook, Iris had no trouble understanding why it was popular with lovers. "The view is magnificent," she said with an awe that was becoming familiar.

Asad might not live in a palace, but his home was one of the most beautiful places on earth.

"It is. I come here to think, to ponder my people's needs in the face of the modernization of our world."

She let her gaze travel over the panoramic vista. Off in the distance, she could see a herd and she bet they were animals cared for by the Sha'b Al'najid. "Seeing all this, it helps you keep perspective, doesn't it?"

"You know me well." He turned to face her, his eyes smiling even though his lips were still.

It reminded her of how he used to be at university.

"I want to." She reached up and cupped his face between both of her hands, loving the feel of his closely cropped beard against her fingers. "I want to very much."

He nuzzled into her touch, turning his head so he could kiss each of her palms. "You do?"

"Yes." She wasn't any good at the games women played with men, and she didn't want to be, either.

If Asad decided he wanted Iris in his future, he would have her as she really was, not something she pretended to be to gain his attention.

He gently pulled her to him, his desert robe enveloping them both. "There is one way you know me better than anyone else."

"Really? No other lovers have learned all your body's secrets?"

"No. You do not know them all though, either, not yet."

"Maybe I could learn some more right now."

He jerked as if startled by her suggestion, but then he smiled. "I thought we both had work to do?" he asked, sounding bemused.

"My work can wait a little. Can yours?" She reached up and kissed the underside of his chin.

He shuddered. "Yes, my dove, for you…for this, it can."

"Good."

"It will be." He started to undress.

But she stopped him. "Let me."

Silent, his eyes darkened by lust, he nodded.

She took her time, removing each of his desert layers with intermittent kisses and caresses until he stood naked before her, the timeless Bedouin sheikh.

She took off her own clothes while he stood watching her, his erection so hard it was nearly parallel to his stomach. They had only made love that morning, but clearly something about this was exciting him beyond bearing.

And then she realized it was the first time she'd initiated the lovemaking since they'd renewed their intimacy.

Apparently he missed her feminine aggression.

She let her last garment fall to the ground and stood proudly naked before him. "I want you."

His entire body shuddered at her words, his nostrils flaring, his eyes narrowing, his gut tightening. Her gaze skimmed lower and she noticed a pearl of preejaculate on the end of his penis. More evidence of sexual desire at its peak. She reached out, swiped it with her finger and then brought the bead of viscous fluid to her mouth.

It was sweeter than when he climaxed, which she

preferred not to swallow. He never seemed to mind, but was always complimentary and grateful when she took him in her mouth at all. Even though he gave her oral almost every time they made love.

One thing he had taught her to appreciate six years ago was that if they both enjoyed it, then whatever they did was beautiful.

She loved tasting him and the way he lost himself to her touch when she took him into her mouth. She felt like he truly belonged to her for those frozen minutes in time, no matter what their future held.

She went to drop to her knees in front of him, but he grabbed her under her arms and stopped her.

"Why?" she asked, not understanding.

He loved this.

"You will hurt yourself."

She looked down at the hard ground and shrugged. "I'll survive."

"No. We will fold my robe into a pad for your knees."

She smiled, realizing the man wasn't turning her down, just taking care of her. "All right."

It took only a moment and then she was where she wanted to be. Wrapping her fingers around his engorged member, she said, "Today you are mine."

"You are not usually so possessive." The bemused tone was back.

She looked up and met his dark gaze. "You don't know what goes on in my head when we make love."

"Perhaps I should."

She just shook her head before leaning forward to lick delicately at the tip of his hardness. He groaned, his hips jerking forward. And she did it again. She loved this game, where she licked and mouthed, but didn't quite take him inside.

After a few minutes of that treatment, he cursed. "You are such a tease."

"Am I? I thought a tease did not follow through."

"My knees will give before you are done playing."

"Poor sheikh…his knees are going weak."

He growled and she grinned and then pushed his foreskin back to take him fully into her mouth. She could never take much of him, he was too big, but she didn't need to. Coordinating the movement of her hands and mouth, she soon had him gritting out a warning that he was close to coming. She pulled her head away to finish him with her hand.

She liked being able to see his face as he climaxed, as well. The ecstasy there always excited her and touched something deep in her heart.

He looked down at her as his body went absolutely rigid, their gaze locking in primal connection. He whispered her name reverently and his ejaculate exploded like a geyser between them. He wasn't inside her, but it felt like their very souls connected in that moment.

"Thank you," he said hoarsely, his eyes devouring her naked body kneeling before him.

She kissed the glistening tip and then licked her lips, the flavor more salty and bitter now that he'd come. "I like it."

"You are a very giving lover."

No. She simply loved him. Someday he would understand that, but she swallowed the words back. It wasn't the right time to admit her emotional vulnerability to him, no matter how close she felt to him in that moment.

She let him tug her to her feet and bring her body flush with his, his expression intent and deliciously predatory. "It is a good thing that my powers of recovery are beyond average."

"I would expect nothing less from the lion of the Sha'b Al'najid."

CHAPTER TWELVE

HE STARTED. "How did you know I am called that?"

"Your name means lion. There's a lion on your bed-spread. It wasn't much of a leap." She was a scientist after all, making deductions based on observations was one of the things she did best.

"My grandmother told you, didn't she?"

She would dearly love to say no, but Genevieve had mentioned it, confirming Iris's supposition. "She said the mantle of lion had been passed from Hanif to you when you took over the tribe."

"My grandfather is still strong."

"But not the primary protector for the Sha'b Al'najid."

"No. That is now my honor."

She rubbed their bodies together delightfully. "Just as it is my honor to give you pleasure."

"You think so?"

"Yes."

"It will then be my honor to please you, as well."

She wasn't going to argue that. Their lovemaking was always explosive and very, very special. At some point, Asad was going to realize what that meant.

They were meant to be together.

He'd gotten sidetracked six years ago, but this time her eyes were fully open, which meant she could help him get the sand out of his when his vision got a little cloudy concerning them.

He made a bed on the ground with their clothing piled under his robe, and still he insisted on her riding him rather than lying beneath him. It wasn't her favorite position, not because it didn't feel good, but when she got lost in the pleasure, sometimes she forgot to move. He helped her, guiding her with a strong but tender grip on her hips, his own body thrusting upward and sending her into panting delight.

His own lust grew faster than she would have thought possible as his eyes fixed on the way her breasts jiggled with her movement. "You are so lovely in your passion, little dove."

Her feminine pride preened under his heated approval, while the bliss inside her body coiled tighter and tighter.

They kissed to muffle their cries when they climaxed, their bodies shuddering in unison. She collapsed on top of him and lay there quietly for several moments of utter contentment.

"This is right," he said.

"Us?"

"Here in the open, with my land all around us, my people tending their herds in the distance."

He liked making love outside. Before coming to Kadar, that was one thing she would never have guessed. She thought it endearing how he considered the land his, though really, it belonged to the country.

They cleaned up with Asad's *kuffiya,* and then returned to the survey site with him wearing only his shirt and loose trousers. He looked debauched and she found she liked the look on him.

When she told him so, he informed her that she

looked sated and that was a look he found pleasing, as well. She grinned in response and took his hand without hesitation when he reached out to her.

When they got back to the survey site, Russell told them that Nawar was still sleeping. Iris felt the need to check on the little girl regardless. When she backed away from the tent after insuring Nawar was still slumbering, Iris bumped into Asad.

He smiled down at her. "You wanted to make sure she had not woken, despite the fact she has not left the tent?"

"She might have realized we were not here—I mean, *you* weren't here—and been nervous about coming out."

"But she is fine."

"Yes."

He smiled, his white teeth flashing. "When she was a baby, I would go into her room at night and lay my hand on her chest to confirm she was breathing."

"I probably would have done the same thing," Iris admitted with a laugh.

"Yes, I think you would have." He brushed her cheek. "You will make a wonderful mother."

She didn't answer, just kept his gaze for several long seconds filled with profundity she only hoped he felt, as well. Then Russell broke the spell, telling her he needed help with a measurement.

Feeling guilty for neglecting her work, Iris sprang to her feet to do so, but Asad grabbed her wrist.

She looked at him with question.

"I am glad you are here."

"I am, too." And she meant it from the very depth of her soul.

She only hoped she'd feel that way in a few weeks

when it came time to leave. If he did not ask her to stay, she wasn't sure she wouldn't beg him to let her anyway.

What was pride in the face of love and the hope of a family?

Asad's phone rang and he picked it up from his desk. "Hello."

He was enjoying a rare day working in his office; Iris and Russell were testing samples in their portable lab.

"Hey, cousin."

"Hakim."

"How is Project Iris going?"

"What do you mean?"

"Oh, come on. You insisted she be the geologist for this study. You don't think I was blind to your ulterior motives."

"I wanted to help her move forward in her career." And maybe he'd wanted her back in his bed, but now... he wanted more.

The certainty had grown with each passing day. They fit in a way he had never done with Badra, and Iris was so good with Nawar. She would be a fantastic stepmother because she understood what it meant to be rejected. Iris would never visit such a thing on a child, but particularly not a child she had shown so much genuine fondness for already.

"And?"

"Maybe more."

"From the way the air sizzled between you even after six years' separation, I'd say a lot more."

Asad had told Hakim about his former relationship with Iris and expressed his guilt for hurting her when he ended it. The king had been one hundred percent behind Asad's plan for some small restitution. Now he had to wonder if Hakim had not seen something all along that Asad had been blind to.

All he said however was, "Perhaps."

"Have you convinced her yet?"

Into his bed, assuredly, not that he would say so to his cousin. But for the more?

"I do not know." He only wished he did, but his *aziz* seemed to make it her goal in life to confuse him.

Hakim laughed. "Good."

Asad verbally encouraged his cousin to do something with a camel that was not anatomically possible.

The king's laughter sounded over the phone again, this time louder. "You deserve a woman who will keep you on your toes. I am glad you found Iris. I cannot even wish you had not screwed up so badly with her in the past—if you hadn't you would not have Nawar and she is a delight."

Asad could not argue with any of that. At one time, all he'd felt toward the very existence of Nawar was anger and disgust, though he'd been loath to admit it, even to himself. But the first time he'd held her, he'd known. He would love that child forever.

He thought it was possible he was in the same boat with Iris, though he wasn't quite ready to admit it… again, even to himself. "I would stand on my head for this woman, but she seems oblivious to my every effort."

"That's quite an admission. Changed your mind about the whole love thing since the last time we talked?" Hakim asked in a tone that said he knew the answer already.

"What are you? A gossiping old woman? Wanting to know my *feelings*."

Instead of getting offended, Hakim's chuckle said he was mightily amused. "What has you so confused, cousin?"

"She will not allow me to call her *aziz*." He'd made the mistake of letting it slip out the night before and he'd woken up to an empty bed, Iris's pillow cold from her departure.

"Catherine wasn't thrilled with me using endearments she didn't think I meant, either."

"But you meant them?" He had to have. Hakim loved his wife fiercely.

"Yes, though it took me a while to realize it. Have you figured it out yet?"

"I have never heard my grandfather tell my grandmother he loves her, but their marriage is as enduring as the mountains." Personally, Asad could happily live the rest of his life without making himself that vulnerable.

So long as it didn't mean losing Iris.

"You don't know what he says in their private moments," Hakim observed. "But more importantly, he has not given Aunt Genevieve cause to doubt him. My esteemed great-uncle treats his wife like she is the queen of his existence and always has."

"I have done my utmost to treat Iris with great affection and care since she arrived in Kadar. I've given up working in my office, put off meetings with important business associates and politicians."

"Does she know that?"

"Naturally not." He did not wish to make her feel bad for the time he made for her.

"How is she supposed to know she's become the queen of your world if you don't tell her?"

"I did not say she was my queen. She will be my lady."

"She's going to be the *Sha'b Al'najid's lady*. You want her to be *your* wife."

"It is the same."

"Don't believe it."

Asad grumbled, "Catherine ran you a merry chase."

"She did and I have never regretted one moment of it, or joining my life with hers."

"You once told me that Catherine had regretted it," Asad said, carefully.

What if Iris came to regret her time with him? She'd made it pretty clear in the beginning that she'd regretted their time together six years ago. Though he knew that was his fault and no one else's.

"It's true. Catherine almost left me once," Hakim agreed, old horror at the thought tingeing his voice. "Do you want to lose Iris again?"

"No." That was one thing he had no doubts about.

"Then you have to convince her to stay."

"I am doing my best." Asad made no effort to hide his exasperation. "She is more than receptive to my lovemaking. She adores my daughter and my grandparents."

"But you are not sure if she still loves you?" Hakim asked perceptively.

Asad frowned, though his cousin could not see it and then sighed. "Does it matter?"

"You tell me."

"What do I do?"

"Tell her the truth, that you brought her to Kadar to woo her into staying."

But even he hadn't known that was what he was doing at the time. Just as he'd been unaware of naming his daughter after Iris. *Self-aware he was not,* he thought cynically. "She's already figured out that I was instrumental in her arrival here."

"Does she know that most of the land she's surveying is owned by your family?"

"No."

"Maybe you should tell her."

"Badra's only interest was in my possessions." He never wanted to see the light of avarice in Iris's eyes.

Not that he would. Intellectually, he knew that, but there it was.

"Iris isn't like that. Catherine and I only saw her for two days, but we worked that out immediately. The geologist will make you a much better wife than your late princess ever did."

"Badra was never mine, no matter that she spoke vows."

"And you were never hers."

The truth of that would have taken Asad's legs out from under him if he had not been sitting at his desk. *"I love her,"* he said with wonder and no small amount of trepidation. His heart and soul belonged to the introverted scientist irrevocably. "I always did."

"Did you really just figure that out?" Hakim asked with disbelief.

"It's not something I thought about." Not until he'd had no choice but to do so.

"Catherine would say that's something you should be telling Iris, not your cousin."

"That I didn't want to label my feelings for her?"

"That you have those feelings for her. I love you like a brother, I really do, but for all your brains, you can be dense, Asad."

"You're right." It wasn't easy admitting, but he had been beyond blind when it came to his feelings for Iris.

If he'd had an ounce more self-awareness, he would never have left her in the States the first time. And that was something Iris needed to know. She deserved the words. "Your wife, on the other hand, is a brilliant woman."

"She is that. She picked me, didn't she?"

"Iris calls me arrogant. I think it's a family trait."

"Catherine is certain of it and is convinced I've already passed it on to our son."

"Not your daughter?"

"My dear wife is convinced that men are arrogant, but women are merely assertive."

Both men shared a laugh at that.

If Asad's was filled a bit with gallows humor, Hakim did not mention it. Blinded by his pride and stubbornness, Asad had ejected the woman he loved from his life—and paid for that choice every day since.

It was all well and good for Hakim to say Asad should tell Iris of his love, but what if she no longer loved him?

She hadn't said the words since coming to Kadar, not once. No matter how amazing their lovemaking. She had opened up to him in the past weeks, but remained adamant he not call her beloved.

Iris never hesitated to spend time with Nawar, but she changed the topic of conversation every time his daughter, or he, brought up the possibility of him marrying again and giving his daughter a mother.

Iris was close to being finished with her survey. And then she would leave Kadar. She never spoke in a way that indicated she planned anything else.

Her joy in her job was apparent, and from what the man who looked and acted more like a brother than an

assistant said, Iris was very good at it. What right did
Asad have to ask her to give it up?

If he did not, what kind of mother would she make
for Nawar and their future children, gone so many
months out of the year? Asad had been looking into
other options for her that would give Iris the opportunity to use her education, but would not take her so
frequently from his side.

What if none of them appealed to her?

What did he have to offer? His daughter, his family,
his tribe…if she did not love them as he did, it would
not be enough.

Had his grandfather felt this fear when asking for
his grandmother's hand?

To ask a woman not of their people to share their
world was no simple matter. After his experience with
Badra especially, Asad had realized his grandmother
was the exception, not the rule.

But then that should give him hope, because Iris
was a special and unique woman in every way, as well.

Iris finished one of the final tests that would confirm
the presence of a semi-precious metal in the area near
where she and Asad had made love outdoors. The
thought of mining happening in the pristine environ-
ment made her stomach twist.

That was the least of her findings, though. Preliminary tests, measurements and observations indicated the existence of rhodium, a rare and very precious
metal. It also demonstrated the probable existence of
aluminum oxide with chromium—or rubies, in lay
terms—buried in the mountains of Kadar.

She said as much to Russell and he frowned. "Your
boyfriend is not going to be happy to hear that."

"Why? Do you think he was hoping for diamonds?" There were some indicators for the stone, but not as strongly as for corundum.

"I think he was hoping for no strong indicators at all. Haven't you two talked about this?" Russell asked, sounding a lot more concerned than she thought he should be.

"No." They'd talked about his work and her career, but not the work she was doing now. "I've avoided discussing my findings because first reports should be made through proper channels to Sheikh Hakim."

"How very professional of you."

She frowned and tossed her half-finger leather gloves in a wadded ball at him. "Don't make fun. It's harder managing a professional and personal relationship together than I ever imagined."

"But you spend every night with him and his family. None of them have mentioned the way Asad feels about mining to you?" Russell asked, sounding like he found that very suspicious, and not a little upsetting.

"The topic has never come up."

"But you *do* talk about your job?"

"About my career as a geologist, yes. Just not this particular survey." She'd never asked Asad what his stance on mining was. She'd assumed it was favorable, since he'd been the one to convince Hakim to bring her in as geologist.

"Sheikh Asad is one of the Middle East's leading conservationist advocates. He is adamantly opposed to overmining, or mining at all when it's done invasively to the ecosystem."

"What? Are you serious?" Asad was an advocate for conservation? A *leading* advocate?

"Absolutely. He's a spokesperson for preserving the desert habitat and with it the Bedouin way of life."

"But how would mining in the mountains impact that?"

"You really think if a mining company comes in, they're going to be okay with a city of tents as the base of their operations?"

"They'll need workers."

"Not Bedouins who are fiercely opposed to changing the landscape. Besides, do you really think Sheikh Asad wants his tribe working in mines? His whole tourist business is based on the Bedouin lifestyle mystique. He's not going to give up his weavers and shepherds to the mines."

Russell's words made sense, but Asad's behavior didn't. Why hadn't he told her he was so opposed to mining?

And if he was opposed, why agree to be the geologist's liaison?

"You don't think…" Russell let his voice trail off. "No, if he doesn't talk about your reports, it can't be that. It wouldn't make sense."

"What?"

Russell shook his head. "A stray thought and a bad one."

"Tell me."

"I was just thinking that if he was opposed to mining, he might get involved with the geologist responsible for preliminary reports that could influence his cousin to go forward with a more in-depth survey, or leave off the idea of mining altogether." Russell looked very uncomfortable with his own thoughts.

Iris didn't find them particularly palatable herself. Would Asad be that sneaky? Her heart said no, but her brain reminded her that he could be ruthless when pursuing a goal.

They needed to talk.

They were bathing together in Asad's family's private spring later that night, after putting Nawar to bed, when he said, "You will be finished here soon."

"Yes, there is one final site we need to take samples and do our measurements."

"I know. The remote location would make traveling to it daily untenable."

"Mmm-hmm," she agreed, her mind still preoccupied by her earlier conversation with Russell.

"Nawar should probably stay behind in the encampment."

That made Iris's attention snap back to the present and what Asad was saying. "But the fieldwork could take a week, or more."

"She will be content with her grandparents."

"She'll miss you."

"You, as well."

Iris certainly hoped so. She would miss Nawar with a terrible ache in her heart. "Why can't she come? We could bring Fadwa to help keep an eye on her."

"Taking a child into the mountains is no simple task. Despite the way others view us, our encampment has many modern amenities we will not have access to in a primitive camp."

"Don't tell me a Bedouin sheikh is afraid of camping with his daughter, no matter how basic the *amenities?*"

"I simply do not want you overwhelmed with the consequences of having Nawar along. She will not be content to be ignored."

"Of course not." And Iris would never do so to the little girl. "She has a right to expect our attention."

"But your job…"

"Will get done. It may take an extra day, or two, but isn't that better than going without her?"

"For me? Definitely. But *you* have made noises about leaving Kadar, I thought perhaps you tired of us."

"I didn't come here to live, Asad. I came here for a job." And she would stay only if it meant being a permanent part of his life, not a temporary bed partner.

"Perhaps you did come here to live, but did not realize it at the time."

Her eyes narrowed. He was making implications she could not ignore. Iris needed it all spelled out though, not left to hopes and assumptions.

Starting with his role as a spokesman for conservation and his very public antimining stance. "You never mentioned that you spearheaded Our Desert Home."

She'd spent her limited time with access to the internet well that afternoon. ODH was a nonprofit conservation organization started by Asad and his grandfather shortly after Nawar's birth. They weren't militant or extremist by any stretch, but Russell had been absolutely right. Their stance on mining was minimal impact, or no mining at all.

"I did not think it would interest you."

"Really?" She wasn't buying it. "I'd think I made my interest in everything about you pretty apparent lately."

He shrugged, looking as if the topic was of little importance right then. That's not the impression she got from his "Message from the Founder" on the website.

He took a deep breath and then met her gaze, his expression stoic. "There are other things I would discuss with you tonight."

If she didn't know better, she'd think he was nervous.

"First, we talk about this. Did you convince Sheikh Hakim to request me as the geologist on this survey in hopes of influencing what I say in my reports?" she asked baldly.

For a moment Asad simply stared at her in uncomprehending silence, but then the storm came. His eyes flashing, his jaw hewn from granite. "You believe I would attempt to get you to lie?"

"No." She hadn't really, no matter how ruthless he could be, but she'd felt the need to ask.

She wanted to hear his denial from his lips. She needed the words, just like she needed other words to change her life.

"If this is so, when have I ever asked about your findings? Or made a move to discourage you from telling anything but the unvarnished truth in these reports of yours?" he demanded, his voice deep with affront.

"I said *no,* Asad."

"Then why ask the question at all?"

"I needed the words."

Asad shut his mouth and stared for several long seconds, and then nodded. "Hakim said you did."

"Hakim knew I entertained brief doubts about your motivation for bringing me to Kadar?" she asked in confusion.

"Hakim believes I should tell you my true motivation for arranging for your visit to my home."

"We've already discussed this." Hadn't they?

"I wanted to help your career. *You* believe I wanted you in my bed again."

"You did."

"I wanted more, though I did not realize it at first. I *want* so much more." His face was flushed and it wasn't from the heat of the water. "I...six years ago I made the biggest mistake of my life walking away from you. I compounded it by marrying Badra, but you must believe I never stopped loving you."

"You loved me?" she asked faintly, so shocked she could barely breathe.

"Yes, but I was a fool and I did not realize it. I had a plan stuck in my head and I did not know how to let it go."

"You loved me," she said again, this time with a tinge of wonder.

"I did. I do." He surged across the pool in totally uncool urgency and grabbed her shoulders, his eyes intent. "So much. How could I not realize it? But I did not. I know now, though. Surely that counts for something."

"Yes, yes...I think it does."

"I hurt you."

"You nearly destroyed me."

"But you were strong...you are strong, so much stronger than I. I don't think I will survive if you turn me away now."

"What do you want?" she asked quietly, hope burning bright in her heart. "Spell it out for me."

Don't let her be making castles in the air again.

"A mother for my daughter. A lady for my people. A wife for myself."

"Are you asking me to marry you?" she asked in choked astonishment, needing to be absolutely certain they were talking about the same thing.

Without answering, he pulled her out of the pool in silence. Drying them both, he wrapped her in one of the thick Turkish robes, and then, wearing a towel tied round his own hips, he dropped to one knee.

He met her gaze, his own so intent, she could drown

in it. "Will you join your life with mine, until the sands are blown completely from the desert?"

That was a long time, a really, really, really long time. She wanted to answer, but her heart was in her throat...or at least that's what it felt like and she couldn't get even a single word out.

"Why...why...I need to tell you why," he said urgently. Though hadn't he already said? She wouldn't mind hearing it again, just to be sure...to know she hadn't been hallucinating. Right? "Because you are truly my *aziz,* my beloved. I loved you six years ago, but was too foolish to acknowledge it. I love you still. I caused us both great grief with my pride and stupidity, but I have taken no other woman to my bed since the month after Nawar was born."

"You've been celibate for the past four years?" she gasped in total shock, the words exploding from her without thought.

He nodded, no embarrassment at the admission in his features. "I only had sex with my wife a handful of times before that."

"But why?"

"You were my heart." He averted his gaze, but then brought it back to her, determination burning there. "I told myself sex just wasn't working because I didn't trust women after the way Badra deceived me, but I'm the one that messed me up. Not her. Yes, she manipulated me, but only because I made it possible. Because I left you when I should have stayed forever."

"You didn't realize."

"I would not admit it to myself, but it was you I wanted when I got my divorce from Badra—and then after she died, it was you I was waiting to claim when the prescribed time for grieving was over."

And he'd hidden it all from himself because he was really bad at admitting what he needed. Maybe because he'd spent a lifetime hiding from the fact he'd needed his parents but they'd chosen to be elsewhere. She didn't know if he'd ever come to see that, but she would make sure from now on that he didn't go without the love he needed from her.

Not ever again. She wasn't ever going to give up on him again, not like she had six years ago.

It was time she admitted that. "I let you go. I didn't fight for you…for us."

"I didn't give you the chance."

"You walked away. I could have walked after you, but I chose to go home and lick my wounds. I was too used to not getting love from the people I needed it most from. I'm never going to be that tolerant again."

"Good," he said fervently.

She brushed tears from her cheeks. "You really do love me."

"With all that I am. Despite my pride, blindness and outright stupidity, God has seen fit to grant us a second chance. Will you take it?"

"Yes," she gasped out as she fell to her knees with him and kissed him all over his face. "I love you, too. So much. I thought I would die when you left six years ago. I didn't want to go back to the States after my survey. I only wanted to stay here with you and your daughter."

"We will never again be parted."

"My job…"

He stilled. "There are other options for a geologist."

"Yes."

"You would consider them?"

"Of course. I don't want to be away from you and Nawar any more than you want me gone."

"You are too perfect for me."

"We are perfect for each other."

"I will love you until the stars no longer grace the sky."

"Show me."

And he did. Magnificently.

EPILOGUE

Iris learned that Asad owned the mountain his grand-father's bathing caves had been found in, and consequently the land and mineral rights to most of the area she'd surveyed.

He was exploring the possibility of mining with minimal environmental impact, but only if it would benefit the Sha'b Al'najid. As he'd told Iris more than once, he was a man who spanned two worlds, the ancient and modern. He saw the need for the mining, both for the benefit of his people and the rest of Kadar, but only if that benefit outweighed the detriment.

Iris invited her parents to the wedding, but the couple had other plans. For the first time in her life, that caused her no pain because she had a plethora of family attending. Asad had bequeathed all his to her upon the announcement of their formal engagement.

Russell came with another female geology student, who shared his taste in humorous T-shirts. They looked in love and Iris was so happy for them. Darren and his family came as well, surprising Iris. She hadn't invited them.

When she asked Asad about it, he told her that the man was her friend and therefore welcome. Still, Iris had been unsure how Asad would react to Darren, but after a quiet talk with the other man, her sheikh had been nothing but the perfect host.

Darren had looked a little pale after the discussion, but said all was well and Iris believed him.

After all, her sheikh was the lion of his people. He had no need to crush another man to prove his worth.

And he never let her forget hers. He loved her so completely and intensely, she could never doubt it.

* * * * *

A sneaky peek at next month...

MODERN™

INTERNATIONAL AFFAIRS, SEDUCTION & PASSION GUARANTEED

My wish list for next month's titles...

In stores from 20th July 2012:

❑ Contract with Consequences – Miranda Lee

❑ The Man She Shouldn't Crave – Lucy Ellis

❑ A Tainted Beauty – Sharon Kendrick

❑ The Dangerous Jacob Wilde – Sandra Marton

In stores from 3rd August 2012:

❑ The Sheikh's Last Gamble – Trish Morey

❑ The Girl He'd Overlooked – Cathy Williams

❑ One Night With The Enemy – Abby Green

❑ His Last Chance at Redemption – Michelle Conder

❑ The Hidden Heart of Rico Rossi – Kate Hardy

Available at WHSmith, Tesco, Asda, Eason, Amazon and Apple

Just can't wait?

Special Offers

Every month we put together collections and
longer reads written by your favourite authors.

Here are some of next month's highlights—
and don't miss our fabulous discount online!

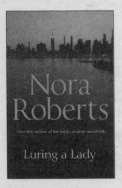

On sale 3rd August   On sale 3rd August   On sale 3rd August

The World of Mills & Boon®

There's a Mills & Boon® series that's perfect for you. We publish ten series and, with new titles every month, you never have to wait long for your favourite to come along.

Blaze®
Scorching hot, sexy reads
4 new stories every month

By Request
Relive the romance with the best of the best
9 new stories every month

Cherish™
Romance to melt the heart every time
12 new stories every month

Desire™
Passionate and dramatic love stories
8 new stories every month